Empire in the Dust

**This Large Print Book carries the
Seal of Approval of N.A.V.H.**

Empire in the Dust

Dan Halacy

Thorndike Press • Thorndike, Maine

Library of Congress Cataloging in Publication Data:

Halacy, D. S. (Daniel Stephen), 1919–
    Empire in the dust / Dan Halacy.
        p. cm.
    ISBN 1-56054-189-X (alk. paper : lg. print)
    1. Large type books. I. Title.
[PS3558.A339E47   1991]   90-17662
813'.54—dc20   CIP

All the characters and events portrayed in this work are
fictitious.

Thorndike Press Large Print edition published in 1991
by arrangement with Walker Publishing Company, Inc.

Cover design by Harry Swanson.

The tree indicium is a trademark of Thorndike Press.

This book is printed on acid-free, high opacity paper. ∞

Empire in the Dust

CHAPTER 1

Frank Cullen sat in the straight-backed pew, arms folded tight across his chest while he listened to the droning voice of the minister. The July heat poured into the church, adding to the rank warmth given off by the congregation. Cullen could see through the nearest window the Texas sky, a pale washed-out blue. As he stared into the cloudless expanse and thought about the months-long drought, the preacher's sermon faded into the background of the cattleman's mind. The words blended into a meaningless stream, but the reverend's thin, almost whiny tone continued to irritate him.

Cullen was still looking out the window, seeing nothing but the shimmer of heated air and the occasional column of dust whirled skyward, when his wife, Emily, nudged him with the red-bound hymnal. Moistening his dry lips, Cullen took the book and searched back in his mind for the number the preacher had called out. With stiff fingers he sought for the page and then held the book close in front of her as they rose together to sing the closing hymn. I am an impostor here, Cullen thought. A godless man, or at least one with a God alien to these people. If there were a God as merciful as the one Emily believed in, would He torture the land with the parching drought the preacher was praying would come to an end?

A thin-lipped spinster pumped life into the gasping organ, and half a hundred dry throats ranged themselves on one side or the other of the melody. Cullen stared stonily ahead until he felt the eyes of his wife burn into his cheek. Without changing expression, he looked down at her.

Emily Cullen was small, almost delicate. Her face appeared little different from the day she married him in Kansas, barring the few tiny wrinkles about her eyes. Yet she was in her forties, as Cullen was, and more than twenty of those years had been spent fighting for life itself in a barren, hostile wasteland. It stunned him that after all they'd been through she still could lift her soprano voice in song and plead with her eyes for him to join her in the hymn.

He had promised himself not to, but he made his lips move for her sake, lifting his head to look beyond the pulpit toward the choir. Marcy was there, the daughter who was all they had for Emily's many and agonized confinements. The girl was slim and straight, half a head taller than the mother who had borne her, and endowed with Cullen's own straight nose and gray eyes. At times, the perfection of her seemed a mockery to him, a thorny reminder that there was no son to carry on his name. Now the thought brought a feeling of guilt, and he sought to banish it from him.

The singers' faces contrasted with the satin robes, and Cullen remembered dully that Emily had bought the material and helped sew the garments. Marcy caught his glance and her head lifted a fraction higher as she smiled tentatively at him.

There was no softening to his face in return. Instead, he shifted his eyes enough to see Shelly Horn, the twenty-year-old settler. Quickly, Cullen dropped his gaze back to the hymnal, feeling intense anger overtake him. For the moment, Cullen set aside the animosity he felt toward Horn's family and farmers in general; it was bitter jealousy prodding his anger now. He and Emily deserved a son like that. A son like young Horn, or better still, George Cox!

To hide the surge of feeling, he sang the last line of the verse, cursing inwardly when the pitch of the tune made his voice break into a treble falsetto. With big fingers, he pinched the book shut, knowing Emily was studying him with concern, but he didn't care. He had come to church. That in itself was enough for a man who knew the folly of praying for rain to a merciless God. Cullen cringed, fingering a letter in his pocket, a letter that could spell the end of twenty hard years of ranching in this tough land.

As if to goad him, the preacher read the Twenty-third Psalm then, lingering over the reference to still waters and the over-running cup. Outside, a gust of dry wind sprayed sand against the wall of the church, and Cullen instinctively turned his eyes away from the window.

"Shall we rise for the benediction?" the preacher asked, raising his hands in an ecclesiastical gesture. "Brother Horn will lead us."

Cullen breathed in air through his nostrils as he bowed his head. If it weren't for Marcy and Emily, he would have walked out of the church as Jethro Horn cleared his throat. Shelly's father was angular and turkey-necked, his skin red against the patched worsted suit. The farmer moved near the pulpit and turned to face the congregation.

"May the words of our mouths, and the meditations of our hearts be acceptable in thy sight, oh Lord, our rock and our redeemer. Amen."

There was a gap of hushed silence, and then a buzz of talk filled the church. Cullen raised his head to gaze full at the farmer who had spoken in his even, restrained tone. There was a quiet power in the lay preacher despite his failure in Trinidad, and now for the first time, Cullen admitted that here was his enemy.

Not Lawson Garrity, the fat, drunken mayor of Trinidad. Not Sheriff Larrabee, for all the way the law turned its back on depredations against the X-R. They were a hindrance, yes, along with drought and plague and rustlers. But the settlers were the ultimate enemy, typified by this sober-voiced farmer in threadbare white shirt, string tie bobbing painfully under his Adam's apple as he talked with friends and neighbors. If the Legislature in Austin had its way, these sodbusters would take over the land.

"Frank?" Emily's hand was moist in his, and he shed his preoccupation with a vigorous movement of head and shoulders.

He took his wife's arm, his flat-crowned hat held loosely in his free hand, and together they moved in the slow line toward the back of the church, which was now populated almost entirely by farmers as the number of ranchers in the area shrank year after year. It occurred to him that they could slip out the side door and escape facing the preacher, but he let the thought pass with a shrug. This would be his last visit to the church, he decided, but he would see it through to the tag end. He owed Emily that much.

"We enjoyed your sermon, Reverend," Emily said, sincerity richening her words as she took the pastor's thin, scrubbed-looking hand. "Bless you."

"Bless *you*, Mrs. Cullen," the preacher said, beaming down at her. "You've done so much for us. Good morning, Mr. Cullen. It's always nice to have you in the congregation."

The hint was there, the gentle reminder that he was seldom at church, but Cullen held himself in, extending a civil hand.

"Good morning, Pastor," he said, looking the preacher in the eye and nodding slightly. Then they moved on and out into the stinging heat of midday.

"You could have said a little more to him," Emily said chidingly. "He's a good man, Frank."

"Yes," Cullen agreed, steering her clear of the crush that clung in front of the church. "I could have said a whole hell of a lot more, but for your sake I didn't." He lifted his hat to his head, and the movement rustled the envelope in his coat pocket as though in reminder.

"Frank!" she said, shocked and looking around to see if he had been heard. "Not on the Sabbath, and at church!"

"Church is over, Emily," he reminded her. "Don't pick at me, not in this heat. Let's get to the buggy."

"Whatever has got into you, dear?" she asked, her eyes puzzled. "It *must* be the heat. I've never heard you — "

"Where's Marcy?" he asked irritably, eager to be back of the team, driving away from the church and Horn and the other settlers. The thought of them made his head ache. Shielding his eyes, he glanced about the churchyard for his daughter.

"Over there, talking to Shelly," Emily said. "Don't rush her — she sees him little enough as it is, Frank."

"I'm out of patience, Emily," he said brusquely. He moved closer to where his daughter and young Horn leaned against the wall in the scant sliver of shade.

"Marcy!" he called, making no attempt to soften his tone. "We're ready to go home."

He saw a red flush sweep her face, and he saw defiance too. His daughter was within an inch of retorting hotly, when the boy stepped back from her, bowing slightly. He held his straw hat in both hands and said something so softly Cullen couldn't catch it.

13

Then Shelly moved toward the church entrance and his parents. Marcy had nothing left but to walk tight-faced toward Cullen.

"I'm not a child!" she protested. "We were discussing choir rehearsal on Wednesday, and Shelly — "

"Shelly, hell!" Cullen said. "I'm sick and tired of hearing about young Horn. Understand?"

"Frank Cullen!" his wife muttered through clinched teeth. "Have you gone mad? I'll not have you talk that way!" Emily's face was tight, and for a miserable moment Cullen was sure she would make a scene in full view of the whole congregation.

"No, I haven't gone mad," he told her, taking her arm and helping her into the buggy. "But I've got a head that's splitting with this damnable heat, and I've heard a bellyful about the Horns. I'm sorry, but that's the way I feel. Marcy, get in."

The girl bit her lip, and color still rode high on her cheeks. But she got onto the backseat without a word, and Cullen swung up beside Emily and unlimbered the whip from its socket. Looking straight ahead, he drove the team out of the churchyard and headed for the ranch.

The horses' hooves produced a dry, clopping sound in the fine dust of the road, and

14

yellow-gray powder caked their sweaty, reeking flanks. With the whip, Cullen kept the team moving at a good clip as they left the town behind them and started up the long rise toward X-R range. To the north, the purple hills floated murkily over the hazy horizon.

As they passed dry tanks and the occasional bloated, stiff-legged carcass of a dead cow, Cullen spat into the road. Overhead, in every direction, the thin blue emptiness of sky taunted him, unstreaked by cloud. It had been so for months, despite the prayers of ranchers and farmers alike. Doubtless, Emily's God would send rain when He relented. Though just what they were being punished for had so far escaped Cullen.

"Daddy," Marcy said suddenly, "I did nothing to deserve the way you acted after church."

"Nothing but make sheep eyes at that wet-nosed son of — "

"Frank! Don't take your temper out on Marcy. What *is* bothering you?"

"You'd rather I made 'sheep eyes' at George Cox?" Marcy asked, her voice spilling hurt pride.

"I can't force you to choose him," he told her grimly. "But you're being foolish to think twice about Shelly Horn. George Cox is a cowman. He'll amount to something, because this is cattle country. Your nester friends can't seem to get that through their thick heads."

"All George sees in me is half of the X-R!" Marcy flared. "He's like this land — hard and tough — and beyond that I see nothing. I'm tired of toughness, Daddy."

"Cox is worth a dozen like Shelly Horn," Cullen cut in, flicking the whip at a heaving rump.

"Do you have to drive them so?" Emily asked. "This is Sunday, Frank. A day for rest."

"I could have got more rest by not going to church," he reminded her. "The sooner I get out of this confounded outfit, the better. And don't tell me how to treat my horses, Emily."

"It's the weather," she said placatingly. "We'll all of us feel better when it rains."

"And when will that be?" he asked angrily.

"When God sees fit," Emily said with forced calm. "We're not the only ones to be hurt by the drought, Frank. The farmers have lost almost everything, but you don't even seem to care."

"Oh, I care," he told her. "It's the one crumb of consolation I have! Maybe now they'll see what I've known for years. Horn and his tribe will go back where they came

16

from. They don't belong, them and their misfit ploughs and wagons. Maybe God is trying to tell them that." It was a logical interpretation, and he turned triumphantly to see tears in his wife's eyes, mixing with the beaded perspiration on her face.

"I don't want to believe you're that heartless, Frank," she said slowly. "You can't be forsaking God."

"Isn't the shoe on the other foot?" he demanded, turning from her to stare at the road that wound down from the ridge toward the X-R ranchhouse two miles distant. "Your precious nesters have been at it only a few years, and they're already licked. You and I have fought this land for over twenty years, and we're stronger than ever. Ever think of it that way, Emily?"

"The more reason we should help our neighbors," she said. "Instead, you fight them at every turn. The Horns are decent people."

"They're farmers who should have stayed on the farmland they came from! I was a fool when I helped build Trinidad. I see that now."

"You mean a fool to help with the church and the school, don't you? Say it, Frank, because I know you're thinking it. All that's important to you in Trinidad is the railroad, the store, your lawyer, and the representative

17

you sent to the Legislature. Say it, and admit you're turning from God!"

"Mother!" Marcy said in strained embarrassment. She leaned forward to put an arm about her mother and looked for a moment at her father, sadness in her young eyes. "We're all wrought up by this heat."

They drove in silence until they reached the home Cullen had built them. The ranchhouse and outbuildings were a fading white that glared harshly in the sun. Even the shade of the cottonwoods did little to temper the parched look of things. This was the worst summer Cullen could remember. Worse even than the ruinous year that had all but wiped them out ten years earlier, and now he ran twice as much stock as then. To compound it, he was committed to buy another herd that would further tax his shrinking supply of water, while the well-drillers were punching one dry bore after another into the parched ground.

Cullen stopped the buggy in the yard and got down. Taking Marcy's hand, he helped her to the ground. She started for the shade of the porch, then looked back at him.

"The choir practice on Wednesday — I plan to go," she said.

"Then change your plans. I forbid it."

"Daddy!" She turned away, lifting her

skirts to hurry up the steps and into the house.

"I hope you'll reconsider," Emily said, brushing aside the hand he offered to help her. "Have you completely forgotten the Bible?"

"No," he said bitterly, determined to see the thing through. "The Bible is fresh in my mind, Emily. Do you remember the passage that goes, 'Bring mine enemies — ' "

" ' — and slay them before me'?" she finished for him, her eyes widening.

"That's *my* God speaking," Cullen said. "I want justice, Emily, and I'll have it."

"But why?" she asked. "What enemies do you have?"

"I think this will explain who my enemies are," he said, reaching at last for the letter in his pocket. "You better include the poor rancher in your next prayers, or we'll be as lost as Jethro Horn and the rest of his kind."

Her face contorted, she took the envelope addressed to him. He left her reading the letter while he walked the team to the barn. Dick Wesp was there, a gimpy little man plaiting a riata he would never use.

"I'll unhitch 'em," Wesp said, getting to his feet, but Cullen shook his head.

Cullen needed time to think, and time for

Emily to understand what was in the message from Congressman Henry Deems. The day had been hard on them all, and he was beginning to feel the full toll of it.

Emily was seated in the swing when he reached the porch, the unfolded letter still in her lap as she moved slowly back and forth. He looked at her, pondering whether to go into the house or not, and she beckoned to him.

"I didn't know," she said. "I hadn't realized it was that serious. Deems sounds worried."

He made a futile noise at the understatement. The legislator was panicking back in Austin, foreseeing the collapse of the big ranches and his own fortune. Cullen reached for the letter and put it back in his pocket.

"I didn't want to worry you," he told his wife, "but this morning everything just came to a head." He sat down beside her, moving the swing creakily for the slight breeze it made.

"Maybe if Deems would back the relief legislation — ?" Emily said.

"Did Austin fret over us in the lean times *we* had?" he demanded. "Was there any relief except what we bought with our souls? They don't *belong* here, Emily. The farmers just don't belong! Why should my taxes underwrite their failure? Where is the justice in the Legislature hitting us ranchers like this?" He touched the pocket that held the warning from Deems.

There *was* no justice in the Legislature's move. The Grange, growing in power, had thrown its weight behind the drive to cut up the big ranches. The same Grange that had been an ardent supporter of a bill that had set aside land for sale when no one else could open up the hard, new country.

"Can they really do it, Frank?" Emily asked. "Could the state go back on a bargain — ?"

"If you make one law, you can make two," he told her. "A man will do a lot to get into power. Deems himself is weakening — you can tell that, can't you? He'll desert me if necessary to save his own hide."

"It was wrong in the first place," she said accusingly. "All that money you gave him."

"Wrong to fight for our lives? Suppose Jethro Horn had been elected then instead of Deems? Do you think he'd have pushed for aid for *me?* I can't understand, Emily. Why do you uphold them over me in everything! It's bad enough I have to fight them, without having my own family against me."

"Maybe I'm wrong, Frank," she said softly, taking his hand in hers. "God forgive me my own mistakes, but I must try to make you see yours. These people are starving, Frank, and we're not. You read what Clara Barton wrote in the Austin papers — they *must* have help. Deems should support the measure because the farmers are his constituents too."

"Should he vote for the bill making me sell the X-R for farmland? Cut it up into plots for fencing, and let land go for twenty cents on each dollar we've spent on it? I'll tell you what wrong is, Emily. It's wrong to be outnumbered! A handful of us ranchers are fighting hundreds of farmers. Farmers who breed snotnose kids by the dozen while — "

He broke off bitterly and stood up, knowing there was no good in his railing.

"Don't blame them for having children," Emily said.

"Why shouldn't I?" he cried out, his hurt naked now. "Don't the graves up there on the hill mean anything to you?"

"*Mean* anything?" she repeated weakly, and he was sorry at once. "You think I can ever forget putting my own flesh in the grave, Frank? But that's not the fault of Jethro Horn any more than it was my fault. The Lord gives, and He takes away too."

"The hell!" Cullen said in a tight whisper. "I've given for too long already. It's my turn to take now, and *no one* stands in my way."

He got up and went out onto the porch. As he looked toward the outbuildings, he saw his young foreman raise a hand in greeting. Without George Cox, Cullen thought, he might have given up the fight long ago.

CHAPTER 2

George Cox watched Frank Cullen turn from the railing and go back into the ranchhouse, then reached into his vest pocket for the sack of tobacco and cigarette papers. He seemed to have found a home for himself in this world at last, he thought as he shook the brown grains onto the translucent paper and pulled the drawstring on the sack tight with his teeth. With his left hand he rolled the smoke, then licked the length of the paper, and smoothed it down. He found a match in Chin Lee's kitchen, lighted his cigarette, and walked slowly back out to the steps and sat down. The sun was high in the sky now but the lean-to roof shaded him from the burning heat.

For the first time in a long while, Cox thought back to the dingy orphanage in Philadelphia. No one wanted to be saddled with a young hellion sure the world was put into being to make his life miserable. At first he had tried hard to do what was wanted of him, but too often he missed the mark and vengeance fell on him like a landslide.

When he turned sixteen, he climbed onto a slow-moving freight train before dawn one morning, not knowing or caring where it was headed. That was ten years ago, and in that time he had come a lot farther than the many hundreds of miles Trinidad was from Philadelphia. He'd shoveled coal on a riverboat and picked cotton in Louisiana, where he learned to ride a horse, and decided he'd be a cowboy. It wasn't easy, but over the years he'd made it. Handyman on a cow ranch near Houston, breaking horses — and his own bones — near Waco, and then the long ride southwest to the X-R ranch near Trinidad where he'd talked Frank Cullen into giving him a job punching cows. On that day, he acquired not only a boss but the closest thing to a father he'd ever had.

Three years ago, that was. And now at twenty six, Cox was foreman of the X-R. He'd had to fight hard to get the position and keep it. He'd had a real knock down, drag-out fight with Skinner Forbes, who'd been in line for the job. Earlier in life, Cox might have killed the man, but with age he was acquiring self-control and discipline, slowly putting the nightmares of his youth behind him. And then there was Marcy, the slender, pretty daughter of his boss. It was Marcy who was the deciding factor in his ambition to become foreman and gain Cullen's respect.

Cox took a last drag on his cigarette and flipped the butt out onto the sandy soil of the yard. Frank Cullen was coming down the steps of the ranchhouse now, and Cox knew he wanted to talk about the coming cattle drive from Fort Worth. Standing up, he took off his hat, ran his left hand through a thatch of dark hair, then set the hat well back on his head. A father-in-law was about the next best thing to a real father, he figured.

"Afternoon, George," Cullen said to his foreman. "You had dinner?"

"Sort of," Cox said with a grin. "Chin is still only about half with us. He gets more out of a bottle than any man I ever knew, and that's a fact."

"One of these days he may go back to China, like he keeps saying," Cullen said, shaking his head. "But don't count on it. You got time to talk about going after those cows up north?"

"Sure do," Cox said. "The deal with Wiggins is still on, then?"

"It is. I got a telegram from him Saturday — if anything he's more eager than ever. Although I couldn't drive him down any on the price."

"It was already a good price," the foreman

26

said shrewdly. "His tough luck is our good luck, I'd say."

"We could use some of that," Cullen said. "The Legislature in Austin is thinking real hard about passing a bill to provide relief money for the farmers. That Red Cross lady, Clara Barton, is there, stirring things up — "

"Damn," Cox said. "I keep hoping those sodbusters'll see they can't make it out here and go back where they belong. This is cattle country, not farmland!"

"You know that and I know that," Cullen said, nodding. "But Congressman Deems is getting scared. He says that farm relief law just might pass, with all the pressure the Legislature's getting right now."

"So?" Cox asked, taking off his hat and resting it on one knee.

"We'll have to take care of that problem when it gets here. Meanwhile, we'll bite the bullet and bring that herd on down here."

"Right, Mr. Cullen. Me and Forbes figure it'll take us three days to ride up there and then about a week to drive 'em down. When do we start?"

"I sent a telegram to Ben Wiggins, saying you boys'll probably be there this Friday or Saturday. No reason you can't ride up on the train — with your horses in a cattle car."

"I guess we could at that, if you can afford

27

it," Cox said, nodding. "It'll save time, and we'll sure enjoy the ride! I should tell you that Forbes has some doubts we can handle another four hundred head — "

"Forbes *what?*" Cullen broke in.

"He's a little short on nerve, I reckon. Says this added load may kill us, short of rain and grass like we are. Don't read me wrong — *I'm* for taking on more cows."

"That's what I want to hear, George," Cullen said, a smile softening the lines of his leather face. "And I won't forget all the help you've been, either. Best foreman I've had out here." He reached over and slapped a hand onto Cox's shoulder.

The praise warmed Cox's insides and emboldened him enough to mention a dream he'd had ever since he realized he had a place on the X-R.

"Mr. Cullen — " he started, but Cullen cut him off.

"Hell, George," the rancher said, getting to his feet. "Call me Boss or Frank or something, will you?"

"Okay, Boss," Cox said, grinning as he stood up and shook hands with Cullen. "Don't think I can handle the Frank yet. But — " He broke off in embarrassment and looked at his boots. This was going to take more nerve than he'd figured it would, even if Cullen was ready to be called Frank.

"But what?" Cullen said. "Let's go up to the house and have a cup of coffee on the porch. It's cooler there."

"I'll get us some from the kitchen. Chin just made a fresh pot. I've got something serious to talk to you about, and — "

"Suits me," Cullen agreed, and stepped onto the porch. "This about money, son?"

"No, sir," Cox said, getting red in the face. "I — I want to ask Miss Marcy if she'll marry me, but first I got to get your permission, I reckon."

"Oh, my," Cullen said in surprise as he swung the door of the bunkhouse open. "That *is* a serious matter, George. Tell the truth, I guess I remember you looking at my daughter a certain kind of way, but I didn't think you were ready to pop the question."

"Well, I am," Cox admitted, following the rancher into the kitchen. "May seem like I got a lot of nerve, but I have a good job here and I know the X-R is going to make it in the long haul. So I'd be honored if you'll give me permission to court Miss Marcy, Mr. Cullen — Boss."

Cullen was silent while he poured two cups of coffee, set them on each side of the table, and waited for Cox to sit down. Then he said "Keeping talking, son."

"Yes, sir," Cox said, nervously stirring sugar into his coffee. "I guess I'm no great shakes as a son-in-law. Never told you much about myself, but I was an orphan as long as I can remember. That was back in Philadelphia. Anyway, my mother must have died when I was so little I don't remember it. There was an aunt took care of me a while, and she told me I never had a father — legal, that is."

"You don't have to tell me all this, George," Cullen said, shaking his head. "I can judge a man by what he does, and — "

"No, I *do* have to tell you. I don't want to pretend I'm somebody I'm not. I never got much schooling. I just wanted you to know I wasn't born to much and that you've pretty well made me what I am now. I've done some bad things in my life, but I've never killed a man or hurt a woman. And I'm asking you if I can ask your daughter to marry me."

"Well, that was a pretty good mouthful," Cullen said, smiling faintly. "But I'll tell you what. I'm no thoroughbred either, George. I ran away — from a good, Christian home — because I was a hellion, too, and in trouble with the law before I could finish school. I've watched you work for a long time now, and you know I like what I see

30

or I wouldn't have made you my foreman. Schooling or no, you've got brains and know how to use them in our kind of work. You're a hard worker, and fair in your dealings. You know cattle well by now, and I think you can take care of yourself in any kind of a situation you get into. I've never seen you drunk, and nobody's ever complained to me about you for any reason."

"Thanks," Cox said, with relief surging in his heart. "Does that mean I can marry your daughter, sir?"

"I didn't say that," Cullen told him with a laugh. "Marcy's got to do the saying, and I sure can't guarantee she'll say yes. But you do have my permission to ask her, and I hope you get the right answer. How's that?"

Cox was on his feet, reaching over to grab Cullen's hand and shake it vigorously. "That's fine!" he said. "Real fine, Boss. I plan to stop in Fort Worth on my way up and buy her a ring — "

"Don't get the cart in front of the horse, now," Cullen warned, his smile fading. "Marcy seems to like one of the boys who sings in the choir — "

"Young Horn?" Cox retorted. "Hell, you know a rancher's daughter's got more brains than to marry a damned farmer! Besides, you and I both know this drought is going to break most of them nesters and send 'em back where they come from. I've been saving my money for a long time, and I have to do it this way. Just so I have your permission to ask her, I'm willing to take that chance with the ring. All right?"

Cullen let out his breath in a sigh and spread his hands. "All right," he said. "Just so you know about young Horn."

"If I can't beat out a skinny farmer with straw in his hair, I don't deserve Marcy," Cox said boldly. "Thanks for your permission, and would you have a drink with me on it? I've got a bottle of good liquor under my bunk."

"My pleasure," Cullen said, and Cox hurried to his bunk. He was back quickly with an unopened quart of whiskey and two small glasses from Chin's cupboard.

He poured a sizable shot into each of them and handed one to Cullen, who stood up, held out his glass, and clinked it against Cox's.

"To success for the X-R — and its foreman," Cullen proposed.

"To Miss Marcy Cullen!" Cox said, his eyes shining. "And thank you, sir. For everything. Bottoms up!"

The X-R's foreman and his crew left for the cattle drive two days later. Cox, Skinner

Forbes (almost as good a man as Cox except for his timidity and a tendency to end up in jail on Saturday nights), and six X-R punchers rode their horses onto a cattle car and then took their gear aboard one of the passenger cars. Cox didn't mention it, but it was the first time he'd paid a fare to ride on a train. This trip was a lot more comfortable too, and to top it off, he won more than twenty dollars playing poker on the way to Fort Worth.

There they bedded the horses down in a stable and got hotel rooms for the night. Cox skipped the party in the saloon that evening and went shopping for Marcy's ring. He bought a sparkly diamond and had enough left to buy the wedding ring too. Later, lying in bed, he thought lovingly of the girl he now had a strong chance of winning. They had danced at square dances, and several times he'd saddled up a horse for her and they had ridden for miles on the ranch. Several times the Cullens had invited him to Sunday dinner — though he was sure Mrs. Cullen did so in the hope of "making a Christian" of him. With Marcy as the prize, he began to think he might even join the church!

In the morning, he had to find which jail Forbes had landed in the night before and get him out. "You know this comes out of your pay, Skinner," Cox reminded him. "Was it worth it?"

"Hell, yes," Forbes said, bleary-eyed but grinning. "Now I'm ready to trail some cows!"

They were riding by noon and had covered half the distance to the Diamond Star by nightfall when they met up with Ben Wiggins and his men driving the herd south. This was rustlers' country but according to Wiggins no problem with as many well-armed riders as they had.

"I'm indebted to X-R," he told Cox. "And you tell old Frank Cullen so, you hear? I can tell you another thing — Cullen's got one hell of a bargain with this herd. We just don't have enough water for this many cows, is all. You better pray for rain yourselves. Here's to a real gulley-washer to fill all our wells and tanks!"

"Amen to that!" Cox chimed in. "And thanks to you Diamond Star people for helping us on the drive."

Later, after a quick tally, he swapped Ben Wiggins the bank draft Cullen had written for a bill of sale for the cattle. The rancher nodded approval as he looked at the amount, and immediately put it in his shirt pocket.

"If it ever rains on us again," he said, "I can buy some more cows with that money.

But right now I just can't take the risk. We been playing it too close for years now, and I'm thinking serious of a ranch up in Montana — where it rains regular. I hope to hell Cullen knows what he's doing. Still no sign of rain down there?"

"If there is, it's pretty well hidden," Cox admitted. "But we'll make out. Got some more wells being drilled, and sooner or later the bottom's going to fall out of that sky. It's just got to!"

"Why has it got to, boy? You sound mighty sure of yourself."

"It's just got to, is all. I got a diamond ring for the lady I'm asking to be my wife. And that lady is Frank Cullen's daughter, Marcy. He gave me permission just a couple days back to ask her. It's just got to rain so I'll keep on having a good job and can afford to build us a nice little house and raise a family. That's why."

"Mighty good reason, son. You like another drink before you hit the bedroll?"

"No, sir — thank you just the same. It'll be a long day tomorrow, and I want to be in shape to push those cows far as we can. Thanks for your help, Mr. Wiggins, and I'll say good night to you."

The drive began early, and by noon they

were well along the trail with few problems from the herd. Strung out for a mile, the cattle moved right along, and Cox smiled his satisfaction as he circled the herd. The Diamond Ranch hands would ride with them more than halfway, although Cox doubted rustlers were bold enough to be dangerous — outside of maybe picking off a few strays.

They bedded the cattle down before dark and ate supper from the chuckwagon Wiggins had sent along. And it was then Cox made the mistake of showing Forbes the ring. It was almost burning a hole in the tobacco sack, and he finally told the older cowboy about his purchase and who it was for. Forbes whistled in amazement when he saw the ring glint in the light from the cookfire.

"You must be got it awful bad, George!" he cried, shaking his head. "You sure Miss Marcy's gonna give you the time of the day — what with the way she looks at Shelly Horn?" That got the rest of the punchers crowding around, demanding to see the ring and expanding on the notion that Marcy Cullen wasn't for the likes of George Cox.

"What do you mean?" Cox demanded, putting the ring away angrily. "I'm her daddy's foreman, ain't I? She's a rancher's daughter, and maybe one day I'll be running the X-R — "

"If this drought don't end they maybe isn't gonna be any X-R!" one of the Star Diamond hands warned. "Ben Wiggins already told us if we got any other prospects we best be cultivatin' them. He's a smart cattleman, and I'm thinking about maybe followin' him up to Montana."

"There'll *always* be an X-R," Cox protested, getting to his feet. "You better talk nice to me, too, or you won't get an invite to the wedding. Time we hit the hay, everybody. Got to be on the way before sunup."

Next morning began the last three days of the drive. Things were looking good, with only a couple cows lost down a ravine when they strayed from the main herd. There was no way to accurately tally this many animals, but Cox and Forbes were sure they'd reach the home ranch with all but a handful of the herd they started with.

"Less'n it comes a gulley-washer and drowns half of 'em," Forbes said. "But that ain't gonna happen. I sure hope old Struthers has punched into some water since we left home."

"He probably has," Cox said with a nod. "And it's got to rain sometime, Skinner.

37

The X-R's been making money for more than twenty years, you know."

"I know it a lot better than you do, bucko," the puncher reminded him sharply.

Well worn, they crossed onto X-R range in midafternoon the seventh day of the drive, pretty much on schedule and still with no serious losses. Cox and Forbes were riding a bit ahead while the other punchers kept the herd together. Reining up for a breather, they watched the dusty cattle pass them knee-high in gray dust. They had watered well that morning, but the tanks and streams here on the X-R had long ago dried up. Cox looked at the sky, trying to seem casual, and Forbes read his mind.

"You're right," the puncher said. "It's sure got to rain sometime. But right now we're driving four hundred head of bargain beef home. Let's worry about one thing at a time, eh, George?"

"I'm not worried," Cox told him. "Let's get up there and get those gates open before these animals run through 'em." He roweled his horse, and Forbes slapped a hand on the flank of his dusty black as they rode up a slight rise and moved ahead of the herd. He saw the settler's wagon just as Forbes swore loudly and leaned forward in his saddle.

"What the hell is that up there?" he cried.
"More sodbusters," Forbes said angrily.
"What are they doing on our land?"

CHAPTER 3

It had been another Sunday like the last one. They ate in silence, Cullen inwardly damning the weather and wondering how Emily and Marcy could manage to look so cool and composed. The heat was striking hard through the toughness that had been his shield for years. Maybe he was getting old, he thought angrily, old and finished at forty-six.

Emily had taken off her apron, and looking across the table it was easy for Cullen to remember the smiling, well-dressed girl entertaining in her parents' home back in Kansas City. Emily could have complained about life on the X-R with good reason had she wanted to, and there were times Cullen wished she would. It would have cut into some of the guilt he felt.

"More coffee?" she asked, and he nodded, holding his cup so that she could fill it from the heavy silver pot she was so proud of.

"Thank you," he said stiffly, the morning's argument still a barrier between them. The women had balked when he told them they were not going into town to church today. Marcy looked at him briefly, and he was aware of the flushed spots high on her cheeks. She was like him in many ways, including her quick temper. She'd have made a fine son, and with a son it wouldn't have been so difficult.

Setting down the cup, he reached for his napkin. A movement in the yard caught his attention, and he turned his head to see a rider dismount and beat dust from his hat as he came toward the porch. It was Skinner Forbes, and shoving back his chair, Cullen got to his feet.

"Excuse me," he said. "The herd must be coming in."

Neither of the women said anything, and he left the room to meet Forbes as the man hit the top step. The horse shuddering at the trough indicated that the puncher had ridden hard, and there was a sober cast to his lined face.

"The herd all right?" Cullen asked. "You look like you been chased clear from the county line."

"Your beef is fine, outside of bein' ganter'n I like to see," Forbes said. "Cox is holding a wagonload of immigrants for you is why I rode in ahead. We caught 'em cutting our fence and butchering prime stock like they'd bought it!"

"Hell!" Cullen said. "These fools won't ever learn. Where's Cox holding them?" Already he was pulling off his tie.

"In the wash a mile south of that gate we put in last month," Forbes said. "About a dozen of the sodbusters. They got lots of sand, too. Youngster went for a shotgun in the wagon, and Cox had to draw on him, said you'd maybe want to set 'em right."

"I do. Wash up, and Mrs. Cullen will give you some dinner. This evening you better go on up to White Tanks and make sure that windmill is pumping. The herd will be dry."

"Yes, *sir!*" Forbes said, grinning and wrinkling his nose appreciatively at the smell of chicken and gravy. The Chinese cook was sleeping off his Saturday drunk, and Cullen couldn't see making the punchers rustle their own food after the hard ride.

He went back inside and down the hall to the bedroom, where he put on the frayed vest hanging on the door and lifted down his gunbelt. The Colt was for show, of course; the fools seemed to understand nothing but strength, and he was glad for George Cox. His foreman would already have put the fear in them.

Emily was waiting for Cullen when he

came back down the hall, eyes narrowed slightly with worry. Before he could stop her, she put both hands up to his shoulders, searching his eyes with hers.

"What is it?" she asked. "Trouble, Frank?"

"No trouble. Cox came on some immigrants with a wagon cutting through our fence and butchering our stock. I'm tired of that, Emily." He pushed her hands down and went by, hearing the crisp rustle of her skirt in the narrow passage.

"Be careful," she said softly. "I hate to see you wear that gun on Sunday, Frank."

"You think *I* enjoy it?" he asked, his voice rising. Marcy still sat at the table, eyes fixed on her plate. "Don't fret over the gun. Just seeing it will put a scare in them. I spent a lot of money on access gates, abiding by the law. Now these nesters can keep *their* part of the bargain, instead of shortcutting across the land like they owned it."

"Will you be back soon?"

"When I can. I told Forbes you'd feed him, Emily. That damned Chin Lee is sleeping it off again."

Emily followed him silently to the porch, waving as he mounted the horse Wesp saddled for him. She didn't like it, but her sympathy for the farmers couldn't blind her to the fact that fence cutting couldn't be tolerated. Even on the Sabbath.

Cullen came to the awkward, highwheeled wagon an hour after he left the ranch. It was where Forbes said it would be, so near the access gate that an oath left his dry lips as he reined up and nodded to the immigrants at the wagon.

"Howdy," George Cox called. The foreman sat in the shade of a rustling cottonwood leaning over the wash, back braced against its trunk. Cox was tall as Cullen, though not yet as big in the chest. Six feet of lean, weathered muscle, with black eyes dominating the sharp planes of cheek and jaw. His Stetson was pushed back, and the expression on his face was one of eminent satisfaction. Cox thrived on the troubles that now frayed at Cullen.

"I see you got the fence mended."

"These hayrakers patched it up," Cox said with a grin. "After they saw the error of their ways, that is."

Cullen turned his attention to the wagon. Three overalled youths stood belligerently alongside it, and a gray-bearded man sat hunched forward on the high seat. Forbes had mentioned a dozen or so immigrants, and Cullen turned to his foreman, the question in his eyes.

"The rest of them are under the tarp," Cox said, nodding toward the tattered covering clinging to the wagon bows. "They got modest when they saw you riding up. Couple women and a flock of kids. Claim they're settling in Trinidad."

"That's right, we are," the youth in the center said, pushing up to his full height and balling his big fists. "Just see you don't ever come to town minus them pistols, cowboy. You may be a big man out here, but I'll sure clean your plough if — "

"Shut up, Will!" The man on the seat looked apologetically at Cullen and rubbed slowly at his stubbled chin. He looked fifty or more, and fear edged the tiredness in his eyes as he spoke. "Name's Palmer. Answer me one question, will you, mister?"

"Go ahead," Cullen said, reining his mount closer. None of the nesters seemed to be armed; the shotgun Forbes had mentioned lay at the base of the tree with its barrel bent.

"You ranchers think you own the county, I reckon?"

"I own what I paid for," Cullen snapped. "The law says I have to let you people pass through, and that's why I put in the gate just north of here. Why didn't you use it?"

"We mended your fence," the farmer

grumbled. "Cutting through saved us two miles or so, and the trail here is lots better."

"You sound familiar with the country," Cullen said sharply.

"Jethro Horn put him up to it," Cox said, untying his mount and swinging into the saddle. "He's the one inviting all these lintbacks out here."

"Keep on," the boy called Will threatened. "I broke a feller's arm for less'n that back home, and — "

"I told you to shut up, Will!" The farmer half rose in the seat and glared down at the boy. "You'd better, or I'll break one of *your* arms." He swung back to Cullen, his red face veined and sweaty.

"Nobody put me up to nothing. There's land out here, that's all I heard. I'm a farmer, mister, a good farmer, and if Jethro Horn figures this land is worth something, that's enough for me."

"Did you bring along irrigation water too?" Cullen asked tauntingly. "It hasn't rained here in months. Did Horn tell you that, farmer?"

"Cows drink water," the man said, working his jaw as though to build up courage. Studying the reins, he went on. "I've heard stories about how you people dam the streams and hog all the water. A cow drinks thirty gallons a day, and you run hundreds of head, and more coming. God gives that water, mister, and — ”

"God don't dig the wells and bank up the tanks," Cullen said. "God don't buy the windmill towers and put fans on top of them. He don't buy sucker rod, either, or pay a driller a dollar a foot for dry holes." He leaned close, wanting to grab the red-faced man by the sweaty shirt and haul him from the seat. "I *don't* dam the river, but I don't let anybody cut in diversion ditches, either. This is cattle country, farmer, and you'll be better off to turn your team around and head back wherever you came from."

"Don't threaten me!" Palmer said. "We got the franchise, and by God I reckon we'll have enough votes to take care of your kind next election. The Legislature is already fixing to — ”

"That's enough!" Cullen roared. He saw the butchered carcass shaded by the tarp now and anger flared at the immigrants' gall. "George, what do you figure that beef was worth?"

"Twenty dollars, at least," the foreman said. "Cutting barbed wire is a criminal offense too."

"They've mended that," Cullen said. "But you can ante up the twenty dollars, farmer."

47

"The hell!" one of the boys shouted. All three of them moved from the wagon in agitation.

"It weren't your brand on that cow!" the farmer protested.

"What's on my land is my responsibility," Cullen told him. "I'm damned sure the cow wasn't yours! Don't be a welsher on top of a thief. Twenty dollars is cheap for that much meat, and you know it."

"We don't have that kind of money," the farmer said, whining now. He was scared, and his eyes flicked from Cullen to Cox and back again. "Honest, mister — "

"All right, George," Cullen said resignedly. "Rope the old fool, and we'll squeeze it out of his hide." As the farmer's boys moved toward him, Cullen unholstered the Colt and thumbed back the hammer. They froze.

Inside the wagon children squalled, and Cullen swore aloud. This was the rottenest part of it. A woman's face appeared back of the seat as Cox unlimbered his rope. The farmer tried to jump off the far side of the wagon, but the loop took him around the chest and jerked tight before he could fend it off.

"Twenty dollars," Cullen said as the woman screamed. "You better think twice, farmer."

"Damn you! I told you I ain't got — "

Cox eased his mount into a walk, and the farmer came out of the wagon seat, hopping awkwardly with his arms pinioned. As he broke into a shuffling run with the tug of the rope, Cox flipped a turn around the saddle horn and flung the remaining coils up and over a cottonwood limb above him. The farmer fought to free himself from the rope, and the woman screamed again, climbing down from the wagon.

The three boys broke, and it took two shots over their heads to stay them this time. Cox's horse walked slowly, and the farmer came free of the ground, howling and kicking his legs as if he thought they'd really hang him.

"Don't kill him!" the woman pleaded, running toward Cullen and tearing at the neck of her dress. Looking down, he saw the crumpled, sweat-darkened banknotes she was offering him and reached for them. He took two tens and gave back the rest. Sobbing, the woman fled toward her husband.

Cox eased off on the rope until the farmer's pawing feet reached the ground. With his wife's help, the man rid himself of the loop and began to rage.

"You'll pay for this!" the farmer bawled. "I didn't believe all the things I'd heard about cowmen, but I do now. By God, you'll pay — I swear to that!"

He clawed at his neck as though the rope had tightened on his windpipe instead of his arms, and hobbled back to the wagon, the hysterical woman clinging to him. She pierced Cullen with wet eyes, and again he cursed what he'd been forced to do. He'd rather fight rustlers than women and children and aging farmers. But there seemed no choice.

"Let it be a lesson," Cox said, shaking out and coiling his dusty rope. His foreman's face was still relaxed, and Cullen envied him that. Nothing seemed to bother him, no chink ever showing in his tough exterior. "Next time you steal beef, take it from a man without a rope and the guts to use it!"

"Now turn your wagon and clear out, Palmer," Cullen added as the farmer mounted the seat. The three boys had climbed into the wagon, the one called Will in tears of rage.

"I'll go back as far as the gate," Palmer said hotly. "Then I'm going to Trinidad and get out a warrant for attempted murder!"

"No!" the woman shrilled, shaking her head nervously. "Let's turn back before — "

"Be quiet!" the farmer told her, shoving her roughly into the back of the wagon. Then he gathered the reins in shaking hands and slapped them onto the rumps of the team.

As the horses completed the swing, Cox drew his gun and fired three shots into the air in quick succession. The animals bolted, and the clumsy wagon crashed roughly over rocks and slewed its butcherknife tires through the sandy wash as they ran in terror. Cox laughed as he emptied the spent cartridges and thumbed in more.

"Give me a good excuse and I'll get rid of him for keeps," Cox said. "Sooner or later we got to start, Boss."

"No," Cullen said. "Leave them be. Where's the herd?" he asked, when the wagon had lost itself in the dust that hung in the hot, still air.

"On the way," Cox told him. "Ought to make White Tanks by night. You got plenty of water there? They're drier than hell itself."

"Unless the windmill gave out, the tank is full. We've kept the other stock away for a week. It was nearly full when I checked two days ago, and I told Forbes to go on up this evening. What did Ben Wiggins have to say?"

"I believe he thinks you're crazy," Cox said, laughing. "Of course, he waited until he had his money to tell me that. He's through, and so is his neighbor, Jennings.

They're selling out and going up to Montana where it rains. Offered me and Forbes jobs even."

"Good riddance," Cullen said, hating the weak ranchers who were pulling out. "Forbes said the stock was a bit gaunt."

"We got our money's worth. They'll fatten. All we need is water. You want to see the herd? We can catch them if we head out now."

"My seeing them won't put weight on them," Cullen said. "Besides, I told Emily I'd be there for supper. I imagine you'd enjoy a decent meal for a change."

"Let's go!" Cox said. "I'm burnt out on beans and dried apples. Hey, this is Sunday again, isn't it? How was church?"

"We didn't go. All those idiots do is pray for rain that never comes."

"We all better pray," Cox said, grinning. "Dead cows stink like hell."

"We'll make it through," Cullen said firmly. "It's going to rain before long, and even if it doesn't, it hurts the farmers more than it does us. Forget Montana, George. When we ship next fall, you'll share the profits, I promise you."

"That's good news, Boss," Cox said. "Marcy still seeing young Horn?"

His boldness took Cullen by surprise, and

he glanced over at the rider beside him. Cox was rolling a cigarette, his face a blank.

"I hope not," Cullen said. "I've told her she shouldn't be thinking about a farmer."

"And she said, 'Yes, Daddy,' I reckon!" Cox licked at brown paper and grinned over the smoke he had built. "What brought that on?"

"A letter from our legislator in Austin. He says that fool running for governor is promising to break the big ranches, and half the Legislature is getting on the bandwagon! With the Red Cross still yelling relief for the farmers."

"Be hell to get *legislated* out of business," Cox said evenly. "We can't let that happen, Boss."

By the time they reached the ranchhouse, a thin haze to the north marked the progress of the herd Cox had bought from the panicking Diamond Star cattlemen. Another four hundred head to add to four times that number already on the land. Cullen was cutting it pretty thin, but there was still enough stubble to see them through a while longer. Water had to be somewhere beneath his acreage so that Struthers wouldn't just keep on punching failure into the sod at a dollar the foot.

Although he tried not to, Cullen looked

53

forward to seeing Marcy and George Cox together at the table. He and Cox unsaddled and he left the foreman in the bunkhouse, cleaning up. Things might break now, if Marcy could just see reason — he'd have the son he had wanted so long, and eventually Marcy would have sons too. Strong sons with the blood of Frank Cullen and George Cox in their veins!

Waiting on the porch, he heard boots crunch across the yard and saw the red glow winking in the darkness. Cox flipped the cigarette away as he came up the stairs and in the faint light from the house Cullen could see the confident smile.

"I brought my appetite," Cox said.

"Good. Come on in."

Emily was there at the table, her face tight, which immediately signaled to Cullen that something was wrong.

"Good evening, George," she said. "I trust you had a good trip."

"Yes, ma'am. Outside of a few sodbuster thieves, no trouble." His voice was crisp and confident, but his face had lost some of its assurance.

"Where's Marcy?" Cullen asked, doubt edging his words.

"She — she has a headache, Frank. It must be this heat. I'm sorry. She said for me to say hello to you, George."

Without a word, Cullen drew out his wife's chair and seated her. Cox waited and they sat down together to eat Emily's supper in strained silence. Watching his foreman, Cullen remembered his mention of Montana. Cullen's anger at Marcy burned deep in his chest.

After the near silent meal, he and Cox went out on the porch and smoked. Cullen apologized for Marcy not being at dinner, but surprisingly his foreman shrugged off his disappointment.

"I guess a woman has bad times with the good," he said. "I'll take a rain check, Mr. Cullen, and you just let me know when Marcy can join us. All right?"

"Sure, George. Soon as we can."

CHAPTER 4

When George Cox had come to the X-R three years back, Cullen didn't pry into what was on the man's back-trail, though he had an idea of what he would have found. That might have been part of his liking for the hand who whipped Cullen's foreman, for good cause, his first week on the ranch.

A man had free choice in his beliefs. He could believe everything at one time or another. Or he could believe in nothing. George Cox seemed to believe in only two things: himself and his job. In a year, Cullen had paid his old foreman off and moved Cox up. Not once had he regretted the decision, even though Skinner Forbes's nose went out of joint. George Cox worked for the X-R with heart, soul, and both his guns.

Marcy had been at school in St. Louis when Cox joined the X-R. She came back, not the child Cullen and Emily had put on the train, but a woman grown. It was then the notion came to Cullen's mind that it might be good for his daughter to marry his foreman. Cox was attractive to women;

Emily herself was impressed until she seemed to lose interest for some reason Cullen couldn't fathom. There was energy to the man, a ferocious vitality you could feel, and at first Marcy too had responded. Cullen had watched them ride together, or sit talking on the porch, biding his time. But after a while she began to avoid Cox, almost as if she feared him rather than disliked him.

Cullen believed the church had been the beginning of the rift. The church and Marcy's singing in the choir . . . alongside of Shelly Horn. Cullen had watched helplessly as his daughter became interested in a young farmer who would likely end his days scrabbling a bare existence from the ground. Cullen was determined his daughter would marry a strong man, a man who saw things as they were and pursued life accordingly. A man like George Cox. But she was as stubborn as her father.

Marcy was at the table for breakfast, looking herself again. In spite of his disappointment, Cullen said nothing of what had happened the night before, and was afraid to speculate on his foreman's feelings. A man, even a patient man, will not wait forever, no matter what the prize.

"More coffee?" Emily asked, and he covered

his cup with a hand and shook his head.

"I've got a lot to do this morning," he told her and stood up. He went outside without speaking to Marcy.

Shadows were still long slants across the yard, but already the heat was there. What Cullen had thought might be a line of cloud beyond the hills to the west must have been morning haze, for now the sky was clear and bright as ever. No wind stirred the branches of the shade trees over him as he crossed to the bunkhouse. Cox still sat at the long table, both elbows propped before him and a cup of coffee held in his hands. He turned at the sound of the door and nodded curtly.

"You want cup of coffee, Boss?" Chin Lee asked, and Cullen told him he did as he sat down alongside his foreman.

"I'll take a couple of men and check the cows you're holding in the hills," Cox said. "There's talk of blackleg north of here, and I don't want to take any chances."

"Not worried about that bunch from Wiggins?"

"Nope. They're all right."

"I brought along that letter from Deems," Cullen said, handing it over. He spooned sugar into the cup Chin Lee set in front of him and stirred it slowly, trying to rid himself of the doubt and worry fermenting in him. Cox never seemed ruffled; Cullen was glad the foreman was back.

Cox read the letter rapidly, a dark expression moving across his features. Pushing back his empty cup, he set down the first page, his face becoming more mobile as he neared the end of Deems's message.

"The bastards," he said at length. "The cottonpicking bastards! We should have been tougher on that bunch yesterday."

"They were just a handful," Cullen said. "We're outnumbered twenty to one anymore."

"Deems is doing damned little for your contributions," Cox said flatly. "I've told you more than once that all these nesters understand is a gun in their bellies."

"We can't gun them all out of the Panhandle," Cullen said tiredly.

"If this relief talk turns into action, you'll wish to hell we had! It'll be like picking lice out of your chaps." Cox handed the envelope back to Cullen and went to get more coffee. "Be hell, wouldn't it?" he said. "Beat by a bunch of filthy hayrakers!"

"Beat, hell!" Cullen said. "They're harder hit by the drought than we are, George. If they stay on, they starve. Even Jethro Horn will think twice before he lets his family in for that."

"Is his boy soprano still warbling pretty in the choir?" Cox got to his feet and stuffed his shirt into his pants, his face a mask.

"He was last week," Cullen admitted, shaken slightly by something in the tone of Cox's voice.

They walked out into the yard together, and Cox tilted his head to scan the sky. Then he said, "I've got something to show you."

Carefully taking the small bag from his shirt pocket, Cox proudly showed the rings to Cullen. The rancher was brought up short by the sight.

"You did get them," he said, forehead creasing as he took the diamond in his calloused palm. "Must have set you back several months' wages, son."

"That's right, sir," Cox told him. "A man don't get married but once, and when he does it he ought to do it right. I reckon you bought Miz Cullen a handsome wedding ring, too."

"I did," Cullen said, nodding his head and remembering when he had been this young and bent on courting a woman. "I asked her ahead of time, though. You remember I told you Marcy is showing some interest in young Horn — "

"You told me," Cox agreed, but he was smiling confidently. "I just can't figure a woman brought up on a ranch like the X-R is going to hook up with a sodbuster, Mr. Cullen. I'm hoping maybe you and Miz Cullen could invite me over to dinner another time — when Miss Marcy is feeling better. So I could declare my intentions to ask your daughter's hand in marriage. You figure that would be all right? Maybe after dinner I could take Miss Marcy for a ride in the buggy — "

"Well, yes. I guess we could do that. Tomorrow evening be all right?"

"Yes, sir! Sooner the better," Cox said excitedly. "I better get myself a haircut before then, I reckon. And get my good coat pressed too. Thanks very much, Boss!"

"That's okay, George. And the best of luck to you."

As Cox went whistling back into the bunkhouse, Cullen turned at the sound of an approaching wagon, surprised to see the boss of the drilling crew. Clad in dirty overalls, Struthers was mopping sweat from his neck with an already soaked bandanna. He was fat, with three chins in successive overlapping folds.

"Hell," he said hoarsely, "when I wind up my contract with you I'm going straight back to Oklahoma where a man belongs, Cullen. This is nothing but a goddam, stinking sinkhole!"

"You're getting paid to drill for water, Struthers," Cullen said sharply. "Don't tell me you've brought in a well already today?"

"I won't tell you that," the driller said irritably. "I ain't brought in nothing, and I won't until that load of stuff shows up from town. I need sucker rod and new bits and — "

"That stuff was supposed to be brought out Saturday," Cullen said angrily. "Why wait until now to tell me?"

"It's a hell of a long ride, for one thing," the fat man said, screwing up his face in protest. "Besides, I figured the teamsters would be out with it today."

Cox came out of the corral on a big gray, waving a hand toward Struthers.

"You got good news for a change, fat man?" he asked, grinning. "We could use some right now."

"Not unless you figure I'm saving you money by not drilling holes," Struthers said. "I was just telling Frank I run out of gear."

"What's the stuff in the wagon?" Cox asked, reining closer to look into the bed of it.

"Junk," Struthers said in disgust. "This

62

is the hardest damned ground I ever saw. Ruins bits quicker'n billy hell. You better get me more wood too, Frank. If I don't get steam up I don't drill no holes."

"How are you fixed for snotrags?" Cox asked. "You want me to go prod those teamsters, Boss?" He sounded eager, but Cullen shook his head.

"No, you go on out and check that herd like you planned. I'll go into Trinidad. I want to send Deems a wire anyway."

"Better put it in Morse code," Cox said with a faint smile. "Or you'll have the town down on you that much more."

"To hell with the town," Cullen said. "Struthers, you want to come along and haul back what you need right now?"

"In this thing?" the driller protested, looking at the battered bed of his wagon. "No, sir! I didn't hire out to do no freighting. I'll get back out to the site. God, I'll be glad to finish up with Texas!"

"See you tomorrow evening, Boss, unless something comes up," Cox told Cullen. The foreman kneed his horse and rode out of the yard, followed by two riders who nodded to Cullen as they passed.

"How does the hole you're working now look?" Cullen asked as Struthers gathered his reins.

"Actually it don't look too bad, Frank. I hit sand just before she broke down this last time. Maybe I got you some water, this hole. If it ain't, you better get you a witching rod or give it up." Hauling on the reins, the driller fought the stringy animal around in a tight circle and headed out of the yard. Cullen watched him go and then walked to the barn.

When he rode by, Emily was waiting on the porch, her face expressionless. Through the window, he could see Marcy washing the dishes and he waved to her.

"Don't wait dinner on me," he called to his wife. "I've got to go see Carl Hertzog."

"All right, Frank. Be careful."

Cullen rode straight and proud, his world rimmed by the horizon in every direction. This burned plain was X-R range; land he had fought hard for in the years back of him. His horse slowed gradually until Cullen spurred him, making the dust splash. The sky was the color of dirty straw, a dry, choking color because of the drought. It was as though Emily's God had marshaled all the evil He could, in one final try to beat Frank Cullen into the parched ground, counting on the years that had gone before to have weakened him. But there was comfort in the knowledge that God was scorching

Horn and the rest of them too.

A mile short of the town, he came on the Horn soddy, a low, ugly mound in the center of bottomland that had once been fertile. In fairness, he had to give the farmer credit. The section had been cleared and ploughed, a rude rail fence surrounding it on all sides. Besides the crops he raised, Horn had for a time run a few head of cattle along with the milk cow and two horses he'd brought with him from the east.

Now there was only a bony horse in the lean-to that passed for a barn. The rest of the stock must have gone into the hungry bellies of the nesters. The garden plot was long withered and lost to the dust, in spite of the barrels of water hauled from the creek near town.

Cullen took his eyes from the soddy and spat into the dust of the trail. Jethro Horn was a fool. A blind, stupid fool without the sense to see he was already finished. But the man clung to some weird vision he must have had when he first came to Trinidad. The dream of a growing town, with himself a power in the running of it. Horn spoke with idiotic faith of a thriving farm community along the river bottom, the land crisscrossed with fence and dotted with white-painted barns filled with dairy cows.

Deep in thought, Cullen didn't see the farmer until he was almost even with him, and the sight of Horn waving his hat startled him. Cullen returned the greeting, but made no effort to slow the horse until Horn spoke.

"Howdy, Mr. Cullen. Do you have a minute to talk?" The farmer spoke in the same proud, deep voice he used in church.

Cullen reined up, surprise crowding out his irritation at being stopped. He had nothing to say that the man would care to hear. But common decency made him reply.

"What's on your mind, Horn?" he asked, pulling the reins to his chest with one big hand. "I've got business in town I want to get to," he told the farmer, looking down past the ragged straw hat to the burned nose and deep-set blue eyes in bony sockets.

"Could you use any help out at the ranch?" Horn said it all in one quick rush of breath, as though that were the only way to get it said.

Back in the soddy, a child yowled and a woman's voice spoke low and soothing. Cullen lifted his eyes toward the sound and then dropped them back on Horn. The nester was *really* hurting! It must have taken desperate courage to ask help from a cattleman.

"I'm full-handed," he said bluntly, rolling the satisfaction around in his mouth. "Sorry, Horn."

"Mending fence, maybe," Horn persisted, the even tenor of his voice breaking now. "Digging tanks, mucking out the barn?"

The man was pleading! For the woman back in the sod house; for his kids and himself. And he was the same man who had campaigned strongly against Deems, vowing to make the country a settler's paradise. His courage galled Cullen in spite of the joy of seeing him beg. These nesters were tough, clinging like ticks to the burned-out land. But there was no purpose to the bravery; only stupidity and blindness. How could Marcy see anything in this farmer's son?

"I've already got my own men doing the chores," Cullen said. It was true; he had pared his crew by several men and made them double up on chores in idle time. "Horn, why don't you get smart and go back?" He nodded to the east, far away down the dusty wind that had risen with the climbing sun.

"Go back?"

"That's right."

"It'll rain again, Mr. Cullen," Horn said, "and we'll be here to thank the Lord. He doesn't forsake His own." He managed a smile then, deep lines forming on his face as though to forgive Cullen and prove there were no hard feelings.

"Suit yourself," Cullen said tightly. "But I have no work for you."

He clucked to the horse, touching the dusty flanks, and then thought of something and reined up again. "A wagonload of immigrants cut my fence north of here, Horn. Killed a cow, too. They were coming to settle, they said. How can you take the responsibility of bringing others out here to starve?"

"I have faith," Horn said simply. "I'm sorry you were so hard on the Palmers, even though they did wrong, as you say."

"I want no fight with women and kids," Cullen said angrily. "All I crave is justice, and I'll see I get it. Grange, church, and whatever else you can throw at me. Understand, Horn?"

"You've made it clear before, Mr. Cullen." The farmer shaded his eyes with a broad, horny palm.

"Fine," Cullen said dryly, and spurred his mount. "Good day."

At the edge of town he came onto the immigrant wagon Cox had stopped on X-R range. Palmer had drawn up in the shade of a tree, and the women were busy over a small fire. They flinched and turned away as he rode past.

He was still wondering about Palmer and the three boys when he saw the knot of men spilling out into the street before the barbershop. He reined up abreast of them, curious as he saw a derby-hatted stranger standing on a chair in the midst of the group. The man was thin, with sideburns down to his lower jaw, and he had hooked his thumbs in vest pockets.

"We can change all that, my friends!" he said loudly. "We're *going* to change it, with your help at the polls and elsewhere. Now — "

The strident voice broke off as the man caught sight of Cullen, still in the saddle. Onlookers turned their heads, following the speaker's gaze, and someone said Cullen's name in a sneering tone. The speaker bent down to catch a whispered message, and his eyes flashed as he looked back at Cullen.

"I understand we're honored with the presence of one of the landed aristocracy, gentlemen. My pleasure, Mr. Cullen, though you'll pardon me if I don't take off my hat to a cattle baron. Let me warn you, sir. The day when innocent men are in mortal danger of being hanged to the nearest tree is finished!"

The sound of Cullen's loud applause cut off whatever was coming next, and the agitator's smile faded.

"Bravo!" Cullen said, dropping his hands. "You talk big, my friend. Maybe you can make it rain, too, and help all of us."

He rode on toward the livery stable, gratified at the hush that lasted until he was well clear of the mob. Then the man on the chair got started again and Cullen knew his victory was shortlived. He found Carl Hertzog in the livery office, playing checkers with a hostler.

"Hello, Carl," Cullen said pleasantly, willing to excuse what might have been an oversight. "I need that well-drilling stuff out on the ranch if I'm going to get any water. You forget to deliver it?"

"Forget?" Hertzog jumped a man to the king row and lifted his glass of dark beer in triumph. "No. My memory is good as ever, Cullen." He smiled at the hostler, still not raising his eyes to look at Cullen.

"What's so damned funny? I'm in no mood for jokes, Hertzog."

"Perhaps because of the meeting outside?" The teamster looked up, unaware of the flecks of foam clinging to the mustache bristling over his lip. "The sheep are beginning to band together. Who will be the goat, eh?"

"I've heard these agitators before. It means nothing."

"We'll see, this time," Hertzog replied crisply. "Have you heard of the Knights of Labor?" He bent again to the board, and something in his manner took away part of Cullen's resolve. Reaching down with one hand, he yanked the man to his feet.

"Get my stuff loaded and out to the ranch, mister. And make it fast, you understand?"

"Let go!" Hertzog said, his voice flat. "Henry! Franz!"

His two drivers moved into the small room, bulky men with muscles big from freighting. The warning flashed sharp in Cullen's mind, and he backed a step from Hertzog.

"What's going on?" he demanded. "You teamsters still hauling goods or not?"

"Yes," Hertzog said. "When you raise our rates to a decent level."

"*Raise* them! Have you gone loco? I'm having a hell of a time paying what you charge now!"

"I can read the papers, Cullen," one driver said. "I know you just bought several more hundred head of cattle."

"So I bought some cows. But I have to sell them to show a profit. You know there's a drought, Hertzog, and it hurts me the same as anybody else. Now is a damn poor time to start talking rate hikes!"

"You'll find us united, Cullen," Hertzog

warned. "Our charges go up five dollars a load from here to the X-R. You can pay it or not."

"I've got cattle that will die without water if I don't get that equipment," Cullen said tightly to the two drivers standing near him. "Then where will any of you be? Now get to work and load up the wagons."

"Load them yourself," Henry Lang said, shrugging. "And don't worry about us. We won't starve." He winked at Hertzog, and the gesture was a challenge to Cullen.

He saw it now, linking a lot of things together. The agitator in front of the barber's, the drive for relief. And now this. Labor had tied in with the Grange, or maybe it was the other way around. Cullen remembered the strife in the East, and the whole thing made a bleak picture. He whirled away from the man at the checkerboard with a curse dying on his lips.

The crowd at the barbershop had grown while he was talking with Hertzog, and Cullen felt fury pound through his veins. He remembered the colossal gall of Jethro Horn asking for work when he must have known this was coming. Perhaps it was the nester's idea of a joke. Bitter-faced, Cullen reached for the reins and put a foot in the stirrup.

"Take off the gun and let's see how brave

you are, mister!"

A handful of men had pulled away from the crowd to walk slowly toward him, drawing on each other's strength and bolstering it with twisted sneers. It was young Will Palmer who made the challenge.

"That's right. We'll see who gets strung up this time, Cullen!"

He turned his back on them and mounted. As he swung up, he saw Mayor Garrity walking across the street, a pompous, paunchy figure in tailored gray broadcloth. It galled Cullen to realize that he appreciated the man's presence now; to admit that his nerves were strung tight by the wave of hatred generating in the minds of a pack of farmers.

"Keep it orderly, gentlemen," Garrity said, his voice crisp with command that was the one thing the army had left him when they stripped him of his captain's bars for drunkenness. "Howdy, Mr. Cullen."

"Howdy," Cullen responded, settling himself in the saddle. "How long have you had the circus, Garrity?" He nodded contemptuously at the crowd.

"It's legal," the mayor said pleasantly. He was enjoying this. "I gave the gentleman permission to speak. It's a free country, you know. Seen Carl Hertzog?"

"I have. It's all of a piece, isn't it? I've

73

always thought you were a jealous man, Garrity."

Anger slitted the mayor's bloodshot eyes and then was gone as fast as it came. He smiled again, anger under control.

"Watch your step, Cullen, and tell young Cox the same, eh? I believe your time of riding roughshod is about done." Without waiting for an answer, the mayor walked over to the edge of the group and spread his arms across the backs of two farmers.

CHAPTER 5

Curbing his temper, Cullen rode down the heat-rippled street to the depot. Dismounting, he left the horse at the log trough and went inside. The telegraph key made a monotonous clicking and the agent looked up slowly from his writing, eyes watery under a soiled paper eyeshade.

Cullen waited for the message to end, blinking his eyes to accustom them to the semi-darkness. The place was foul with the stink of stale cigars, but the coolness was a relief from the sun and he was glad for the respite.

"Howdy, Frank," the agent said when the key before him finally went silent. "Hotter'n hell, ain't it?" Theo Leggett had been in the station since the railroad came to Trinidad; he was pushing sixty now and seldom traveled further than his own platform except for his meals and an occasional drink at Gilliam's.

"It's hot," Cullen agreed, leaning his elbows on the railing that split the inside of the depot. "I want to send a message to Henry Deems in Austin."

"Write it down," Leggett said, nodding toward a soiled pad. "I can read it better if you print it big, too." He grinned and scratched a match along the side of his trousers to relight the dead stump of cigar in his mouth.

Cullen wrote with the short lead pencil hanging on a string by the pad. It was brief, but it said what he wanted it to: WE ARE HANGING ON. SURE TO RAIN SOON. STOP WORRYING AND DON'T DESERT ME. He signed it simply "C" and turned the pad around as Leggett shuffled to the rail.

"Get it out right away, will you?"

"I'll do that," the agent said, tracing a dirty fingernail across the message and moving his lips with the words. "Everybody's wiring Austin lately. That'll be two dollars."

Cullen put the silver dollars on the rail and straightened. He doubted that what he had written Deems would get back to the Grange; Leggett owed the farmers nothing and the crusty agent was independent as an ancient mossyhorn. Not that it made much difference.

Cullen's horse looked up alertly from the trough at the sound of his boots on the slats, but he went past the animal and halfway down the block on foot. The weight of heat striking him had changed his mind about riding out of town just yet. A beer might cut some of the dust away and ease the trip back to the ranch.

Gilliam's place was nearly deserted, as it usually was on a weekday since the drought. A chunky drummer sat at a table to the back of the saloon, and a swamper hummed nasally while he sprinkled down the floor with damp sawdust. Paul Clay, the sheriff's deputy, stood at the bar with an Austin paper spread before him and a glass at his right hand.

The lawman glanced up self-consciously, nodded to Cullen, and went back to his paper. Clay had tried farming a half-section in the bottoms and given it up in less than a year. He was single and seemed decent. Uncommunicative, he had said maybe a dozen words to Cullen in the last six months, and he added nothing to that now.

Ramsey Gilliam came from the back room, a towel over his shoulder, and moved slowly to the bar. His smile was pleasantly professional; he had run the saloon for six years and kept on good terms with town and ranchers alike. The Scot had found his place in life and seemed to enjoy it. He sold beer and whiskey, and likely made a cut of the girls' take. To do it, he steered a course between valor and discretion.

"Afternoon, Cullen," the man said cheerfully. "Haven't seen you for a while. What's your favor?"

"A beer," Cullen said. "And if it's cool, I'll drink two."

"Right." Gilliam drew a glass, raked the foam from the top, and slid it down to Cullen. Then he drew another for himself and leaned sociably across the bar.

"You're not too busy," Cullen observed.

"No," Gilliam agreed, glancing around the dim saloon. "Everybody's listening to free speeches."

"It's a free country," Cullen said acidly. The beer was cool, and he savored it on his tongue and the back of his throat. When it was gone, he wiped at the mustache of foam with the back of his hand and regarded the white beads of it clinging to dark hairs.

"That tasted like more."

"This one's on the house," Gilliam said. He refilled the glass, letting the head stand this time. "I got to cultivate my paying customers these days." He said it easily, his mustache wrinkling with his smile.

"Thanks. I'd think you'd sell a barrel of this a day, with the weather like it is."

"If I gave credit I couldn't ship it in here fast enough," Gilliam said with annoyance. "But I don't give any more credit — until it rains."

Cullen finished the beer and ran his tongue softly around his moist lips. He couldn't feel any effect from the beer but its taste and a pleasant fullness in his belly. He put a quarter down on the bar, and Gilliam raked it in and smiled.

"Come back," he said. "Meantime, pray for rain with the rest of us."

Sunlight and heat enveloped Cullen again like a smoldering weight, and he gasped involuntarily as he went from the roof's shade into the street. Half-shutting his eyes against the stinging glare, he didn't see the team until the animals nearly ran him down.

"Whoa there!" the wagon driver shouted as Cullen flung up an arm and jumped awkwardly into the clear. It was Shelly Horn, standing up in the highwheeled wagon to haul on his lines.

Cullen's sudden leap had lifted his hat from his head, and it spun into the dust, almost under the wagon wheels. Cursing, he sprang to retrieve it.

"Damn it!" he shouted. "Watch where you're going with that baling-wire rig, you young hayseed!"

The boy's face, a thin, tougher copy of Jethro Horn's, colored as he looked back at Cullen. He straddled the seat, the team under control, and his voice was even despite the slate hardness of his eyes.

"You own the street too, I reckon?" he asked. "Pa's against profanity, but I think he'd understand why I'm telling you to go straight to hell, Mr. Cullen!"

Turning, he clucked to the team and drove on, the narrow tires of the wagon biting deep in the dust and leaving the double, slicing track Cullen had come to hate. The wagons were a symbol in his mind, like the nesters themselves. Misfits, built for farm country, they nevertheless hung together perversely, rattling across the Panhandle in increasing numbers.

Cullen got his horse and rode slowly from town, grateful for not having to pass the still-assembled mob of farmers. Rolling his shoulders forward, he let his body slump tiredly in the saddle. When the Horn soddy came in view, he left the trail and angled to the north to avoid tangling with any of them. Although his anger was subsiding gradually as the heat's lethargy gripped his mind, he couldn't trust himself with the six-gun bulking his hip. Cox had been right a long time back. They had let the nesters go for too long.

There was no peace either in the thought that he had been wrong in cursing the Horn boy. It hadn't been the incident itself that made him lose his head, but all the things back of it. Now, with time to consider, he was amazed at the farmer's courage in facing him. Sand, Cox had called it. The settlers were doing more than just hanging on lately, pressuring the Legislature for help, and now this satin-voiced agitator moving in from God knew where to set up shop on the streets of Trinidad!

Hertzog. The man was a skunk! Freighting for the X-R and the other ranches had built the teamsters to where they were now, but there was no gratitude or even appreciation for that fact. Instead, they were playing both ends against the middle, seeing a rise of farming in the area if Horn and the rest hung on.

What Hertzog wanted now was blackmail, plain and simple. If Cullen paid, there'd be more pressure every time he was in a bind. The teamsters were smart, seeing Cullen with his back to the wall. The continuing contracts they had with the military — hauling to the fort — would see them through until they could tell which way the battle was going. If the ranchers went under, they could switch whole hog to the farmers and likely be glad to see it happen.

It was a rotten choice left for Cullen. Much as it hurt, he would have to put his own men to packing out equipment and wood for Struthers and his crew of drillers. Supplementary cattle feed would have to be hauled the same way. With the crew already cut to the bone as it was, they might balk at turning teamster on top of everything else.

Cresting the rise, he lifted his head enough to see the ranchhouse shrinking low under cottonwoods as if to escape the battering heat. Beyond it, clear to the opposite horizon, the sky stretched tight and taunting with still no hint of rainfall. Instead, it sucked the moisture right out of the ground. He felt his flesh prickle with the dryness and swore aloud. The thought came of what he would do if he lost cattle heavily this year and the bank pressed him for cash. Ben Wiggins wasn't the first to run, and the worry still nagged that Cox might be tempted by the Montana job. Especially with Marcy acting the way she had. Almost as he thought of the girl, he saw her through the kitchen window as he rode toward the barn.

Marcy was still in the kitchen when he came in from splashing his dusty face with water from the pump. This time he'd have to reason with her.

"Evenin', Marcy," he said.

She turned from the stove, a smudge of flour on her pink face.

"Hello, Dad!" She blew a strand of straw-colored hair aside and smiled at him. It had been some time since their row over Shelly Horn, and Emily had likely talked to her about it.

"I'm sorry for riding you so hard about young Horn," he said with an effort. "I was wrong to do that."

Her face flushed as she listened to him and she began to shake her head. "I understand, Daddy," she said. "But I have to do what I think is right, too — "

"I know you do, little girl," he agreed, calling her that old nickname for the first time in ages. "So I'm backing off. You're a woman grown now — I should have realized that all along, but you know I've got problems, honey."

"Maybe I'm selfish," she offered uncertainly. "But — "

"You're a good daughter," he told her, putting his hands on her shoulders. "And I can't tell you who to marry. But I want you to hear George Cox out when he comes to supper tomorrow evening. The poor boy has already bought you a ring as big as a marble, Marcy, and — "

"Oh, he hasn't!" she cried, frowning. "Why would he be so confident when he's never said a word to me, Daddy?"

"A man in love don't do much thinking, daughter," he told her. "I tried to reason with him, but he's gone ahead and spent a lot of money — and now he's asked for permission to court you. Will you do me the favor of just sitting still and listening to him when he comes tomorrow, Marcy? I don't hold out much hope you're going to say yes to George, even though I wish you could."

There were tears in her eyes now, and she was shaking her head slowly to kill what little hope he had. But she nodded bravely in answer to his question.

"Of course I can do that," she said, reaching into her apron pocket for her handkerchief and mopping her eyes. "You know I like George, Daddy. I'm sure he's a good man but — "

"Thank you, daughter," Cullen said, hugging her to him for the first time in longer than he could remember. "That's all I ask of you. And I'll say no more against Shelly Horn."

It didn't go nearly as well with Emily, who had come in behind him quietly as Marcy disappeared down the hall toward her room.

"You know she won't say yes to George Cox," she said, shaking her head and frowning at him.

"And I didn't tell her to do that," he retorted defensively. "George is ten times the man young Horn is, and you can't blame me for hoping Marcy will see the light."

"That's not fair," Emily said. "Farmer or no, Shelly is a fine boy — "

"Emily, listen to me. That damned young hayraker nearly knocked me down with his team today, and cursed me out when I called him on it!"

"Who cursed first?" Emily asked without looking at him. "You're a stubborn man lately, Frank. Those people are near starving."

He snorted, wanting to tell her what else had been engineered against him now, but something kept him from it.

"It's nature's law," he said, filling his plate and keeping his eyes down. "They've failed. Let them go back where they came from. Help them this year, and next year there'll be twice as many asking for relief! This is cattle land, Emily, and you know it."

"Is it, Frank? I want you to do this thing — for me, if you will — but do it. Write to Deems, throw your strength back of help for them. If the measure is enacted it could help us all."

"Good God, Emily! Was there relief for *me* the year we burned? Or the times the three of us ate potatoes for weeks? I tamed this wilderness, Emily. With wells and tanks I did it. It's survival, pure and simple, and they don't belong here, them or their damned wagons!"

Suddenly the idea came to him full-blown. The ungainly wagons, desperate drivers — there was the answer to it all, and he hadn't even seen it until Emily spelled it out for him!

"Frank?" His wife watched him with quick concern. "Are you all right?" She got the coffeepot from the stove and refilled his cup, her hand resting lightly on his shoulder as she did.

"All right?" he echoed. "I'm *fine!*" He got up from the table, stilling her questions with his excited words.

"You want me to help Horn and the others, Emily? Well, I'll do it for you! I'm a fool for not thinking of it sooner, and I thank you for correcting my mistake!"

"Frank — " She stopped in confusion at his sudden change, and he leaned over and kissed her lightly on the cheek.

"I'll be back in a while," he said.

In spite of her worried protest, he left her in the kitchen. Glad that he hadn't mentioned Hertzog's ultimatum and what was back of it, he settled the still-sweated hat on his head and yelled to Wesp for a fresh horse. He rode out of the yard oblivious to the dust and heat. Here was the perfect solution; he could dump it in Horn's lap and watch him squirm. The farmer was begging for work, and Emily was after Cullen to help them. If Horn turned it down, fine. If he didn't, Horn would have plenty of work if he was man enough to do it.

He found Jethro Horn in the shade of his lean-to, filing patiently on a boulder-nicked plowshare. The farmer looked up in surprise at the interruption and laid aside the file.

"Afternoon, Cullen," he said through thin lips, his eyes filled with worry. He looked toward the sod house and then back at Cullen. "Is it about the boy? He mentioned a set-to with you — "

"No, I didn't ride five miles to gripe about your kid over some trivial thing. You asked a while ago about work. You still want it?"

Horn looked at him dumbly, the words apparently triggering no response at all. And then he nodded, his beard moving with the up and down tilt of his head.

"You're offering me a job, Mr. Cullen?"

"Yes, that's what I — "

"Pa. Supper's on the table." The girl didn't see Cullen until then, and her mouth went shut at the sight of him. She put a hand to the neck of her thin dress where it spread wide for the sake of coolness. Horn's daughter was a year younger than Marcy, but she had developed faster, and now she was full-bosomed in spite of the thin face and arms.

"Tell your mother we'll have company for supper, Trissa," Horn said, recovering his composure. "You will do us the honor, Mr. Cullen?"

Cullen shook his head. "No, thank you. I'll just be a minute with my proposition." It galled him that the nester could outdo him in manners, but Cullen's tight pride wouldn't permit him to sit down with the farmer's family. Pride, or maybe it was conscience.

"I told you I'd do anything," Horn said. "That goes even more now. Our youngest is sick, and there'll be the doctor to be paid."

Temptation was strong in Cullen to drag out his pleasure over the spot he had Horn in, savoring it like strong liquor. But he overcame the impulse and gave it to the nester straight.

"I'll hire you to haul stuff from town to my ranch," he said. "Gear for Struthers's crew, and wood besides. And probably feed for my cows."

"What of Hertzog?" Horn asked, brows

pinching and his voice uncertain. There was a weary flatness to his expression now as the realization grew of what Cullen was offering.

"Hertzog has been listening to the pap the Knights of Labor are doling out on street corners," Cullen said. "Don't pretend you didn't know he's trying to stick me for a five-dollar hike in rates. I can't pay that, and my crew has enough to do, handling cows."

Horn dropped his eyes to his big knuckles, and one hand squeezed the other until the joints popped dryly. Sweat had darkened the wool undershirt he wore, and the rag around his throat was soaked. His body gave off a rank smell that came across the space between them as Cullen watched the functioning of Horn's mind.

The nester knew what it meant, and must be probing the hard cunning back of the offer. If Horn hauled for the X-R, he'd be splitting the solidarity the Grange and Labor counted on. Besides helping Cullen, he'd be courting the hatred of Hertzog and others — even his own people. The gauntlet he'd run would be murderous. When Horn looked up, all this was in the blue eyes. He appraised Cullen with that stare, and guilt was bitter in the rancher's parched throat. Even the knowledge that Horn had a choice helped little. Part of the sweetness of his victory soured as they looked at each other.

"I don't figure you'll do it," Cullen said. "It would be no picnic." He was challenging the man, daring him to refuse. And Horn took the bait.

"How many wagons can you use?" he asked. He straightened, lifting an overall strap back in place. Erect, he was an inch taller than Cullen and probably as hard-muscled.

"Two rigs should do it," Cullen said, knowing he had his man now. The torture of the decision was in Horn's eyes, a decision dictated by hunger. "You can put sideboards on them and report to the station agent in the morning. I've got to make up as fast as I can for Hertzog dragging his feet."

"I'll need some authorization, won't I?"

"I'll be there," Cullen told him. "You want an advance against your wages?"

Horn shook his head, pride drawing at the muscles in his stringy neck.

"You can pay me when I deliver," he said. "Same rates you paid Hertzog?"

It crossed Cullen's mind that Cox would have squeezed the farmer as hard as he could, but he put the thought aside. He wanted justice and no more.

"That's right. And you've got yourself a job as long as you can hold it. I'll see you in the morning."

"Thanks, Mr. Cullen," Jethro Horn said, and the twisting currents of emotion were plain in the sun-scalded face. "I'll be there." His expression was that of a man forced to peddle his principles for bread for his family.

Riding out of the place, Cullen smiled to himself. A dry, bitter smile of triumph. The tide was turning now.

CHAPTER 6

Instead of going back to the ranch, Cullen rode for Trinidad. If he didn't spend the night in town, he'd have to get up at three in the morning to be at Hertzog's in time. Besides that, he wanted to be alone for a while — to think everything through before he saw Emily again.

He ate in the hotel restaurant, had a whiskey in Gilliam's bar, and then went to bed at about ten. He hadn't told Emily he wouldn't be back to the ranch, but business sometimes kept him out. She would understand. The drink helped drive worry from his mind, and he stretched out on the hard cot and slept with little difficulty.

The rattling of the early train woke him, and he swung his feet onto the floor, not sure for a second just where he was. After dressing, he went down the hall and got hot water and a razor from the clerk. It was still fairly cool, and he hoped with little conviction that the breeze out of the north was bringing rain.

Sheriff Hayes Larrabee was eating when

Cullen went into the restaurant, his deputy, Paul Clay, across the table from him. Cullen nodded and went on by, planning to sit at the counter, but Larrabee motioned to him with a friendly gesture.

"Hell, Cullen, sit down with us and pass the time of morning! Don't see much of you anymore." They scraped their chairs, making room for him, and the waitress took his order.

The coffee smelled of chicory, but it was hot and helped burn away the greasy taste of the eggs. Restaurant food always drove home the fact that Emily was a fine cook, and he wondered if it might have been better to get up at three after all. Larrabee watched him quizzically, busy with a toothpick.

"What's the occasion?" the sheriff asked. "You catching a train to Austin, maybe?"

"Try again," Cullen said, smiling and adding more sugar to his coffee. "You're getting nosy in your old age, Hayes."

The deputy looked embarrassed at his tone, but the sheriff laughed loudly.

"It pays to be nosy, Cullen. Takes a politician to hold down a law job anymore. What the devil *are* you doing in town?"

"Right now I'm finishing a miserable breakfast," Cullen told him. "When I get through, I'm going down to the station and see that my stuff is loaded for the ranch."

"You agreed to terms with Hertzog already?" Larrabee's voice was relieved.

"You better come along," Cullen told him patiently. "I'm not sure of all the details myself just yet." He got up and put a half-dollar on the table. Then he turned away from the sheriff and went out into the street. Crossing in a long slant, he came to the feed barn.

"Morning, Mr. Cullen," the hostler said, rocking his chair forward from the wall. "I'll get that horse saddled right away."

"Never mind, Bob. I'll do it. He might be skittish. Put it on my bill, will you?"

He saddled and rode for the station, grinning faintly when he saw the sheriff and his deputy walking in the same direction. The wagons were already there, Horn's and one other. Horn was scattering the ashes of a small fire. Cullen was almost on top of the wagons before he recognized the second driver. It was Palmer, the newcomer he and Cox had forced to pay for the butchered beef, and a frown crossed his face.

"You have a change of heart, Palmer? Last time I saw you there was a threat of squaring things."

The man cleared his throat and looked uncomfortable, seemingly afraid to say anything. Horn spoke for him.

"I'll vouch for him, Cullen. Fred Palmer is my cousin — it took every cent he had to get here. He knows how things stand."

"All right," Cullen said, as the sheriff came alongside. "I'm paying you the same as Hertzog. But anything lost or damaged will come out of that."

"Nothing will be lost," Horn said dryly. "I hauled a load higher than my head clear from Missouri in this wagon. Fred did the same."

"Fine." Cullen shouted for Leggett, and the agent came out of the depot in his undershirt and trousers. "Let these men load up with my stuff, and I'll take the bill of lading."

"You know what you're doing?" Larrabee asked. The friendliness shown at breakfast was gone, and now there was worry lining the sheriff's face.

"I think I do," Cullen told him. "They call it strikebreaking in the East. Why?"

"Hertzog," Larrabee said. "The freighters won't like it, Cullen."

"I'll bet you're right."

"You're pretty shrewd, Cullen. And pretty rotten. You've bought yourself some starving men. Their blood will be on your hands, not mine."

"Blood?" Cullen said, raising his eyebrows with innocent enjoyment. "There'll be no blood. This is a business deal, pure and simple. No concern of yours."

"I didn't think you'd pull a stunt like this."

"What makes me any different from the rest?" Cullen asked. "I've come to you about rustling a dozen times and got nothing but a slap on the back and the information that you can't police the whole country. Larrabee, you look one-sided as hell to me — did you know that?"

"What you're setting up is murder," Larrabee said hoarsely. His face was flushed with more than the morning heat, and his breath came fast and heavy. "Them drovers won't take this lying down."

"You're the law. Protect the nesters."

"Damn you to hell," the sheriff said thickly and reined off. "I hope this mess blows up in your face, Cullen. I swear to God I do!"

Cullen looked over his shoulder with pleasure as the sheriff rode away. What had begun as simply a last-ditch choice was a kind of sweet satisfaction now. With this one move he had settled things with them all. With Horn, Hertzog, and the whole town — the nesters in particular. He had the ringleader and one of his close friends both dependent on him now for a living. His row with Emily would be resolved too.

It was mid-morning when he reached the site where Struthers was drilling for water. The fat man was working on his steam boiler, and he nodded when Cullen told him the gear was on its way.

"It's about time," Struthers said. "You got your own men freighting now?"

"No. I put a couple sodbusters to work and won myself a star in heaven. Fellow named Fred Palmer is coming here." He had told Horn to make the longer trip up to White Tanks with sucker rod and barbed wire.

"All right. I'll have you some water shortly. If that stuff gets here."

"It will," Cullen told him.

There was the smell of chicken from Emily's kitchen as he rode into the yard, and he smiled at the thought of a good meal to wash away the taste of his greasy breakfast. Wesp limped from the barn and led the chestnut over to the trough before Cullen pulled off the saddle.

"You look like you got some good news, boss," the ranch hand said.

"Maybe I do," Cullen replied. "It's about time, don't you think?"

He went into the kitchen and hung his

hat on the wall. Emily turned from the stove and he smiled at her.

"Just in time for dinner," he said pleasantly. "Smells good, Emily. Plenty for George?" He was tighter inside than he could understand.

"Of course," she said, bringing a steaming platter from the oven. "We missed you last night. I waited supper till all hours."

"Sorry," he said. "There was something I had to tend to in Trinidad."

"You mentioned helping Jethro Horn — "

"That's right. You're always after me to help them out, so I did, Emily. Horn and another nester are hauling out the stuff Hertzog left at the station. The teamsters are trying to squeeze me and I won't take it."

"You didn't, Frank!" she said, shocked. "You wouldn't pit them against each other that way!"

"It's all right when they line up against me, I suppose?" he asked angrily. "And besides, what guarantee do you have that there'll be trouble? If they're all such honorable men, what makes you think they'll turn against each other? I'm a little tired of your interference, Emily."

The other hands gave Cox a bad time of it as he got ready for dinner with the Cullens.

"Don't you look nice!" Skinner Forbes teased. "Hair slicked down, shaved, and foo-foo water on your face. Never knew you had a frock coat, George!"

"Lot of things you never knew, Skinner. You can wish me luck or not, I'm gonna come back here and make all you punchers green with envy."

"You want to bet something on that?" Forbes said with a taunting grin.

"I'd bet you ten dollars if you had ten dollars," Cox told him disdainfully.

"Here's my ten — you're covered! And I got plenty of witnesses to the bet, too."

"Anybody else?" Cox demanded belligerently.

"Nobody else has any money left," Forbes told him. "You better get on over to the ranchhouse, George. I see the wagon coming through the gate right now."

Cox walked up to the house, where he was greeted by Mrs. Cullen.

"Good afternoon, George," Emily said to him, smiling a little as she showed him into the parlor. "We're so glad you could join us for dinner."

"Thank you for the invitation, ma'am. I do appreciate it."

"Hello, George," Frank Cullen said, putting out a big hand. Emily excused herself and left the two men alone. "Good to have you with us again. Marcy's helping her mother get the table set, so we've got a few minutes. How about a glass of wine? Elderberry wine — Emily made it herself."

"Thank you, sir. A glass of wine sounds good."

Cullen poured two ornate wine glasses half full, and they touched rims and sipped at the sweet liquid until Mrs. Cullen called from the dining room.

Marcy was more beautiful than he'd ever seen her, Cox thought as he held her chair for her and then eased it in toward the table. She smiled at him pleasantly and his spirits rose as he thought of the ring in his vest pocket. He even said "Amen" when Cullen said grace.

"Daddy tells me the drive went very well," Marcy said as she passed the mashed potatoes. "We do appreciate the fine work you're doing for us."

"Thank you," he said happily. "I reckon that's what I get paid for, though. Your daddy's right — we only lost a few head — " He had almost mentioned the beef the sodbusters had butchered before he caught himself. Instead, he said, "Would you like to ride out to the White Tanks and see them? Good looking cattle they are."

Marcy seemed to hesitate a moment, darting her eyes quickly from her mother to her father, and then she nodded. "That would be nice, George. If we can be back before dark. I have some things to do — "

"Won't even take that long," he said, smiling with relief that she had said yes. Surely Cullen had at least hinted at why his foreman had been invited to dinner this afternoon. "You'll probably want to take along a parasol — "

"All right," she said, and smiled. "Thank you for suggesting it. Can I pass you the sweet potatoes?"

"Yes, ma'am," he said. "I love sweet potatoes."

They talked easily during the short buggy ride out to where the new herd was watering at the well Struthers had brought in just in time. Cox had been afraid he might panic, sitting right next to her, smelling her perfume. But it wasn't like that at all. She spoke right up, reminding him a little bit of Frank Cullen himself. She was not only the most beautiful woman in the county but probably the smartest as well!

He helped her down from the buggy, and she snapped open the parasol and walked with him to the clump of shade trees near the watering hole. Closing the parasol, she looked up at him and said, "Daddy said there's something you want to tell me, George."

"Yes, Miss Marcy," he said, his hand going unconsciously to the ring in his pocket. "I want to ask for your hand in marriage — " It came out so easily he couldn't believe he had said it. But he was shaking enough that he put out a hand to steady himself against the stunted tree. Marcy looked away from him, lowering her eyes. For a minute, he thought she was going to cry. But an offer of marriage might be enough to bring a woman to tears, he thought.

"I want to marry you, Marcy Cullen," he repeated his proposal in simpler form and watched her lift her face toward his, her eyes now seeming soft in a sad sort of way.

"I'm honored," she said, so softly it was almost a whisper. "I've known you for some time, George, and I have great admiration for you. Daddy says you're a fine foreman, and that in time you will probably have a ranch of your own. Ranching is all I've known, and so our interests are alike — "

Emboldened beyond his hopes, he reached suddenly into his vest pocket and brought out the diamond ring. Holding it gently in his right hand, he held it out to her. "I already have a ring," he said, not mentioning the solid gold band he had also bought. "I'll be the happiest man in the county — "

Suddenly she was biting her lip and shaking her head as she looked up at him. The joy in his heart froze suddenly into ice, and he felt his hand close fiercely around the diamond ring.

"I can't marry you, George," she said barely above a whisper. "I've always thought of you as my good friend. But — I don't love you, can't you see? I love someone else — "

"Not Shelly Horn?" he said unbelievingly. "You said you loved ranching!"

"I do. Very much. But I also happen to love Shelly Horn. I'd love him whether he was a farmer, a rancher, or a drummer. Can't you see?"

"No," he said, his voice sounding as hollow as if he were talking down a well. "No I can't, Marcy."

"George," she said gently, reaching out a hand to his arm. "I like you fine — but I *love* Shelly. Please understand — "

"Damn!" he said thickly, and looked at the sand under his feet. He put the ring back into his pocket automatically and then wiped his hands together before dropping them to his sides. "I guess that settles it, then. I'll take you home."

As he turned toward the buggy, she said, "We haven't looked at the new cattle yet, George. There's still plenty of time — "

"I've seen them cows," he said bitterly. "All I ever need to see them, I reckon. I'll take you back to the house."

They walked the few steps to the buggy, and he gave her a hand up, then climbed in himself.

"I'm so sorry, George," she said in a soft voice as they headed back down the slope toward the ranch.

"I'm sorry, too," he told her. "Very sorry. But I guess that's that, isn't it."

He left her on the porch of the ranchhouse and drove the buggy to the barn. Then he shed the frock coat, saddled his own horse, and rode fast for Trinidad, relieved that none of the hands had come out to ask how the proposal went.

Cullen had trouble sleeping after Marcy told him the outcome of George's proposal. He hadn't expected anything better, still he was disappointed. It didn't help any that Emily was angry about his using the nesters to haul equipment and was sleeping in the parlor, leaving him to toss all night. The next morning he dressed quietly and walked across the yard to the bunkhouse.

"Hey, George!" Cullen called. There was no answer, so he went into the bunkhouse and called again. Cox was snoring in his bunk, and when Cullen went closer he caught the reek of whiskey and cursed. Cox lay across the bunk at an angle, his boots touching the floor. Cullen kicked hard on one of the soles.

"Wake up, George. Come on man, snap out of it!"

The foreman grunted, rolled bloodshot eyes, and shut them again as he tried to turn over in the bunk. Cullen caught him roughly by one arm and hauled him into a sitting position.

"What the hell is the matter with you?" he demanded. He hadn't seen Cox drunk for over a year and then it had been in Gilliam's and with a reason.

"There's not a damned thing the matter with me," Cox said sullenly, jerking his arm free. "I got likkered up — you mind?"

"Don't talk to me that way," Cullen snapped, "or I'll think you're still drunk. Douse your head and go on up to White Tanks. There's a load of freight gone up there."

"The hell," Cox said, shaking his shaggy head to clear it. "Did Hertzog back down?"

"I don't much care if Hertzog ever backs down. I got Horn hauling for me now. Him

105

and that fellow Palmer we sold a cow to."

"Well, I'll be double-damned," Cox said, a bitter smile wrinkling his whiskered face. "You didn't!"

"Everybody's telling me that," Cullen said. "But I did it all right. All the high and mighty principles I've heard so much about went down the drain when the bastards got hungry enough. We'll see how those soapbox agitators do from here on in."

"Best news I've had all month," Cox said, getting up and walking painfully over to the mirror tacked to the wall. "Only it comes pretty late."

"I still want to know how come I find you sleeping off a drunk."

"You can't be that stupid," Cox said, turning around quickly to face him. "I asked your daughter for her hand and got it — right across the face. I'm no fool, Cullen, not anymore. There's nothing for me here, never was. And now you're hiring those hayrakers. That caps it for me, I'm going to Montana."

"Because your feelings are hurt?" Cullen said desperately, seeing everything begin to collapse. "Can't you see why I hired Horn? I've split them wide open now — no matter how it goes, we win! And as for Marcy and the Horn boy — "

"Save your breath, Cullen. I'm leaving. She can have the hayraker, and raise his snot-nosed brats. The X-R ranch is through, I can see that."

"You're making a mistake, George. We'll come out of this on top! And I'll sell you part interest on credit."

"The hell! I know what the X-R is to you. It *is* you, and it will go to your daughter when you're done. You don't fool me, Frank Cullen, so don't waste the breath." Cullen recognized the hatred born of hurt, the consuming fury that could craze, and he pitied the man standing before him. Worst of all, he feared his foreman spoke the truth. Slowly Cullen turned and walked from the bunkhouse.

He had Cox's pay ready when his ex-foreman came out. Shaved and looking human again, Cox got his own horse, saddled, and swung aboard.

"I owe you this," Cullen told him, and handed up the money. Cox took it and scanned it with narrowed eyes, noting the amount. Vicious pride showed as he threw it in the dirt at Cullen's feet.

"You owe me a hell of a lot more than that," he said, and rode out.

Cullen's world was coming apart slowly

as he watched Cox disappear into the hills north of the ranchhouse. On stiff legs, he walked to the corner of the corral and leaned against the poles. He took a cigar from his pocket and wet it with his tongue. Striking a match with his thumbnail, he lit the stogie and sucked in pungent smoke, but there was no pleasure in the taste. His body was strung too tight, and his empty stomach protested. There was only the sigh of breeze in the cottonwoods and the faint, metallic sound of Wesp's harmonica.

A man made plans, and the plans fell through. Nothing had worked the way it should, and he wasn't alone in failing in his dreams. George Cox harbored a bitter hurt too.

For a long time, he fought the urge to saddle and ride north after Cox. But Cullen threw himself into the day's routine. That night he worked on his books until he heard the sound of horses and went to the porch. Wesp came limping from the barn, and both of them moved across the yard together as a wagon came around the turn and along the corral. Jethro Horn was hunched forward on the seat. Cullen frowned in surprise.

As the wagon neared him, the driver cried, "Whoa!" in a thin raspy voice. "Mr. Cullen," Horn began, "I — " And then his voice

108

108

broke, and he pitched forward as Wesp shouted a warning. Together they caught the man, bracing him and easing him down.

"What the hell, Horn!" Cullen cried in irritation. "Has the heat go you or — " He saw it then, the bloody hole in the nester's hickory shirt. The bullet had caught him square between the shoulder blades.

CHAPTER 7

At first, the thin creaking of wagon wheels was part of Shelly's dream, and then the noise pulled him from the ragged sleep he had finally managed. The familiar creaking sound came from their wagon; his father was back from the hauling job Cullen had given him. Shelly swung his feet to the floor, rubbing a calloused palm against the drawers that clung tight to his thigh muscles, and wondered if he should get up or feign sleep. His pa had looked whipped when he drove away from the place before daybreak.

Shelly knew Cullen was a wily devil to pit the men he fought with against each other. And yet Cullen had begot a daughter like Marcy. The thought of the girl made him ache to see her.

Outside, the wagon sounds ceased momentarily, and then harness leather slapped through the warm blackness. Shelly shook his head to clear it and stood barefooted on the rough floor. Beyond the thin partition he could hear his mother's measured breathing, her sleep that of one who can accept a miracle from any source. There was no sound from the back room; the two girls were asleep.

He would walk out to the barn and talk with his pa there. Guiltily he thought of the food the money would buy, the shoes that would let Trissa go to church. Pa had said it wasn't money, but the love of it, that was the evil, and — The sound of running feet brought him up short, and he frowned. A fist was banging hard on the door.

"Shelly! Shelly Horn!" The door swung in then, and the shock of hearing Marcy Cullen was so great he forgot he was in his underclothes and barefoot. Through the open door, the sky was lighter enough than the inner darkness that he could make out Marcy's silhouette and the wagon beyond her, bouncing toward town.

"Marcy — "

"Shelly, hurry!" Her voice was low, almost husky, and he knew suddenly that she was crying; had been when she ran to the door. "Your father's been shot!"

"Oh God!"

He didn't know he had said the words; there was no feeling in his throat, no consciousness of his lips moving. But he gripped her shoulders tight for a brief moment in the silence after his exclamation. His fingers felt thick and puffy, and there was no meaning in the touch of her hands along his arms. Wanting to retreat back into the safety of the dream he had just left, he broke away from her and started pulling on his shirt, overalls, and shoes.

There was a scratching sound back of the partition, and a flare of light that made jagged shadows and patches. His mother's voice, sleep-filled and tremulous, came to him.

"Jethro? You back safe and sound?"

As she came into the kitchen holding the lamp ahead of her, Marcy Cullen made a soft, swallowing sound and moved across the room toward the thin woman in the patched shift.

"Marcy Cullen? Shelly, what — "

"It's Pa," Shelly said, knowing it had to hurt. "He's been shot. I got to go to him."

"Shot? Jethro — No! No! Oh God!"

Shelly jerked his head up at the piercing wail. His mother would have dropped the lamp except that Marcy was there to take it from her and put it on the table. But the girl wasn't strong enough to hold the older woman up.

"Ma!" Shelly sprang forward, the sobs cutting him like a dull knife. "Don't *cry* like that, Ma!" Together he and Marcy lifted and carried the slack form to the cot.

"Shelly! What's the matter, what's happened?" It was Trissa, standing in the door to the back room, one hand catching her nightgown together under her throat. Yellow hair hung in disarray about her shoulders, but fear had driven the sleep from her face. Back of her, Billie Jo peered with the wide-mouthed astonishment of an eight-year-old, her face still feverish.

"Your pa is dead!" Sarah Horn's voice rose in keening terror. "God strike me down for making him do it!"

"Mrs. Horn, please. He *isn't* dead. Daddy's taking him to the doctor!"

"Don't you touch me! Shelly, don't leave her touch me. She likely helped do it!"

"Ma, stop it," Shelly said harshly. "You straighten up so we can go help Pa, you hear?"

"God is visiting destruction on me, don't you see it? I had a dream, Shelly. I had a dream plain as day. It was your pa's birthright I made him sell. I — "

"Catch her!" Trissa almost screamed. "She's going to faint!"

Billie Jo was crying in terror now, and Shelly was afraid his head would split wide open. When his mother subsided on the cot it was a relief; it gave him a chance to think sensibly again. Marcy put words to his thoughts.

"You'd better ride into town with Daddy, Shelly," she said. "Before — "

"I'm going," he said, bending to lace his boots. "Trissa, you get Ma's smelling salts and take care of her 'til I get back. Marcy, you reckon you could stay and help out?"

"Of course, Shelly. That's why I came." There was compassion in the girl's face, and she bent to chafe the unconscious woman's wrists. "I'll be praying until I hear."

"Billie Jo!" He left the harshness in his voice in an attempt to get through the fear in his small sister. "Stop that yelling and go get Miss Cullen a glass of tea, you hear? You're the one who's always wanting company, so you treat her nice."

Billie Jo blinked in surprise through the shiny tears and then nodded, seizing eagerly on something she could understand. She ran across the room to the cupboard and lifted down a Mason jar filled with strong tea. Shelly rubbed a hand through her tousled head as he passed on his way to the door.

"Keep Ma down, Trissa," he yelled back. "If you have to tie her down. Goodbye, Marcy."

He ran to the barn, whistling for old Ben as he went. It was the first time Marcy Cullen had come to call, he thought bitterly. He had been a fool to ever even think about the girl twice, he could see that now. The lines of battle were drawn, and Marcy Cullen could belong nowhere but in the enemy camp. Not bothering with a saddle, he led the old horse out of the sagging barn and pulled himself up. Then he rode to town with the weight of bitterness a heavy black lump in him and tears drying in the wind as fast as they formed in his eyes.

"God give me strength," he said when the lights of Trinidad rose out of the darkness, marveling that the prayer could come at all. He would need strength in the time ahead.

Jethro Horn's wagon sat in the street in front of the doctor's house, the team still shuddering from the run. Half a dozen men leaned against the fence near the gate, their voices dropping as Shelly swung down and ran past them. There was lamplight etching the windows and glass panes in the door a bright yellow, and Shelly tried to make that mean something. As he grabbed for the knob, the door swung in. The doctor's wife had a wrapper about her nightgown, and her face was impassive.

"My father," Shelly said, choking the words around his thick tongue. "Is he — "

"In here," she said, leading him toward a door off the hall.

It was bright inside, with light reflecting from the lamps against the mirrors the doctor had set up. Jethro Horn lay on the operating table, shirt and underclothes stripped away from his chest. On the far side of the table Frank Cullen and his wife looked up at the sound of Shelly's entrance, and the doctor turned from his job of bandaging. His voice was tired and angry.

"I told you I didn't want anybody else in here, Zona." Then he blinked in recognition and nodded his head. Straightening, he pinched at the bridge of his nose tiredly. There was blood on his arms. "I didn't know it was you, son."

"Pa," Shelly said. "Pa, it's me, Shelly. I got here quick as I could!"

There was a flicker of the craggy eyebrows, but the eyes didn't come open. Thin blue lips moved, but no sound came. In desperation Shelly grasped at his father's hand, and the cold of it went through him like ice.

"Pa," he said softly. "Listen, Pa, you can't die now! We've stuck it out too long. You hear, Pa?" His voice trailed off, and he felt like he was going to vomit. He must have been watching when the spirit flickered from the worn body, but there was no way to tell. Maybe his father hadn't known he was there at all.

Shelly had passed out once when he was little: one time when he hit his leg with the butt of the axe, and it was that way now. The sweat on his forehead was like drops of ice, and his stomach twisted in on itself. When the doctor pulled his hand from his father's, Shelly had to fumble against the wall for support. Then it passed, before anybody had to help him, and the jagged streaks of light and dark stood still so he could focus his eyes. The doctor was pulling a sheet over the dead man who had been his father.

"I did all I could," Frank Cullen said, from the corner of the room. "I bound him up tight as I could, Doc."

"I know that, Cullen," the doctor said. He turned down the lamps so that the shadows on the wall lost their sharpness. "Where he was hit God Almighty couldn't have helped him. I sure couldn't." He let his breath out in a long sigh, and his eyes flicked across Shelly and back at the corpse.

"Who did it?" Shelly asked, his voice hollow with the misery in him. When you got to be a man it wasn't like you figured at all. When a man got scared there was no place to hide.

"I don't know," Frank Cullen said; the irritation in his voice belying the apologetic

117

working of his mouth. "He pulled into my place with that hole in him. I don't guess he knew himself who shot him."

"I know who caused the killing, though," Emily Cullen said quietly.

"That's enough!" Cullen snapped. "You were the one wanting to help these people — "

"Your hands are unclean, Frank," she said, keeping her voice down. "You knew something like this would happen."

"I knew no such thing! By God, Emily — "

"Don't blaspheme, Frank. If you want to hit me, go ahead. I have to say what I know is true. You've turned on God and your fellow men, and for that I beg Shelly's forgiveness."

She moved toward Shelly, and her arms went around him before he realized what she was doing. When he flinched she drew back, then he fended her off roughly.

"Don't touch me, ma'am. You hear? Don't ever touch me!" He heard his voice going high and fought for control, remembering his mother's hysterical condemnation of Marcy. The split was complete now.

"We'd better get the sheriff, Cullen," the doctor said. His wife was at his elbow with a cup of coffee, so hot the steam wreathed it like smoke. About to lift the cup to his lips, the doctor replaced it in the saucer and proffered it to Shelly. "Here, son, you better sit down and drink this."

"I don't want nothing," Shelly protested. "Nothing but my shotgun."

"Please don't, Shelly," Emily Cullen said, her eyes pleading. "Let the law take care of this. Reverend Burton will be here soon — wait and talk to him."

"I don't need the reverend," Shelly said harshly. "An eye for an eye — it says that in the Bible."

"You can see the sheriff, Doc," Cullen said. He moved toward his wife, the look on his face that of a man who has made a mistake and doesn't know how to right it. "Right now I've got to get my wife and daughter home."

"Go on without me, Frank," Emily Cullen said, the look she flashed at him shaking Shelly. "My home isn't with you anymore."

"Don't be a fool!" Cullen lashed out. "Hell's apt to break loose in town any minute!" He tried to take her arm, but she twisted free.

"Go on, then. Run while you can, Frank. The Horns will need help. That's where I'm going."

"We'll make out," Shelly said stiffly. "We don't need help from you." The thought of Marcy back at the house twisted in him, made him less sure.

"At least take me to my daughter, then," the woman said. "We'll work out something."

"Emily." Cullen didn't try to take his wife's arm this time. "I'm sorry, Emily. I'll rent a buggy, and we can stop by for Marcy on the way home."

"It's too late to be sorry," she said tightly. "Too late, Frank. All the cattle in Texas aren't worth what's happened now."

"I didn't kill him," Cullen said wearily. "I'll see the man hanged who did."

Shelly turned to the doctor, who was drinking the coffee slowly now. The man's eyes were tired, and his hand shook slightly.

"About the — funeral," Shelly said, trying to keep his voice steady. "I don't know how — "

"The reverend will be here shortly, son. You go on home and get some rest, and come back tomorrow. I'm — sorry." He dropped his eyes to stare at his cup, sloshing the coffee in it absently. As if an afterthought, he went on. "Mrs. Cullen, Zona and I can put you up here tonight, if you'd like."

"I'll go with Shelly, if he'll take me," Emily Cullen said determinedly. "It's going to be hard on his mother."

The knot of men at the gate broke apart for them as they came out. Shelly recognized

Hicks the barber, hat in hand. The tall man cleared his throat self-consciously before he spoke.

"We sent for Larrabee. Is Horn — "

"Jethro Horn is dead, gentlemen," Emily Cullen said. "I'm sure the law can apprehend his killer."

"I'm sorry as can be, Shelly," someone in back mumbled and the barber nodded. But none of it helped with the hurt inside Shelly.

"Come on, Miz Cullen," he said gruffly. "I want to get back."

She must have known he was crying, because halfway to the place she leaned over and patted his arm gently.

"The Lord *is* our shepherd, Shelly," she said. "We shall not want."

She kept on with the psalm to its end, and after that she just talked to him, with her hand still on his arm. He would have told her to stop, except once he looked down and saw that she was crying, too. He drove the wagon right up to the door, and his mother was framed in the lamplight when he helped Emily Cullen down from the wagon seat.

"Ma," he said, because he knew no other way. "Ma, Pa is dead."

He shut his eyes as the first scream knifed into his brain, and he couldn't watch as Trissa and the two Cullen women fought his mother back into the house. Without Marcy and her mother it would have been worse. Or maybe it would have been better. Should he be spared any of the hurt, he wondered.

In the barn he unhitched Ben, then stumbled outside and leaned tiredly against the barn. It had been perhaps two hours since Marcy pounded on the door, but he felt an age older. Of their own accord, his legs buckled and he slid down to a sitting position, not moving even with the pain of a sharp edge of board grinding into his shoulder blade. The sound of sobbing in the house covered Marcy's footsteps so that he didn't hear her until she knelt in the dirt and manure before him, one hand reaching toward his face.

"Shelly?"

He turned his head until his cheek pressed flat against the board. In the sky he could make out part of the Dipper, and off at an angle the polestar, and he fixed his eyes on them to have something to hang onto.

"Shelly, I'm so sorry."

For a long time there was no sound except from the house. He wanted to hurt her the way he was hurt, and he cursed himself inwardly for that.

"Shelly, come in and try to get some sleep. Please."

"Go away," he said. "Leave me alone, Marcy."

CHAPTER 8

Cullen slept poorly, despite his tiredness and the strain of what had happened. Twice in the night, after he had managed to doze, he woke when his fumbling arm encountered the emptiness of the other half of the bed. His curse rang hollow in the darkness of the room, and loneliness rankled him. He heard a rooster crow before he went to sleep again, and when he woke, half-sick to his stomach, light filtered in through the curtains at the window.

He thought the thing through again, from start to finish, as he dressed. There was no other way it could have been, no thing he should or should not have done. In the kitchen he laid a fire and stropped his razor while the water heated. There had been a light in the bunkhouse last night when he rode in, but he hadn't wanted to talk to anyone about what happened until he straightened it out in his own mind. The shooting and Emily's reaction were like a bad dream; a dream that made no sense at all in the light of day. Tightness in his muscles dragged the razor clumsily, shifting the angle so that he cut himself twice before he finished.

He considered fixing himself something to eat, or at least coffee, but abandoned the idea. There was no place for pride or appearances now. The men would know sooner or later, and there was no point in putting it off. Drying his face, he looked out the window toward the bunkhouse. Earl Wesp was limping from the barn, and there was the smell of coffee and bacon. Cullen would eat the Chinaman's cooking and discuss things with George Cox — if he had come to his senses and ridden back to the ranch. Half his mind still clung to the plan he had held for so long; the plan that Shelly Horn had wrecked for him.

There were four men at the table when Cullen entered the bunkhouse. Wesp and Skinner Forbes, plus Cob Durham and Joe Whitehead, who must have come in from the Tanks. The two with their backs to him went on eating noisily until Forbes spoke. George Cox hadn't returned, and Cullen knew he'd been foolish to hope for that.

"Morning, Boss. I hear you had some excitement around the place last night." Durham looked half-around and nodded to Cullen as he moved to the end of the table.

"You hear right," Cullen told Forbes,

straddling the short bench. "Horn died right after we got him to the Doc. Hey, Chin. Bring me some coffee."

"I'll be damned!" Durham said, a sheepish look on his flat face. "Trissa'll take that hard." The rider had once squired the nester girl to dances in town, Cullen remembered.

The dull thudding of hooves outside turned his head; maybe half a dozen horses or more, and coming fast. Cullen slid off the bench and headed for the door, agitation churning the hunger in his belly to nausea again. He shoved the screen door open in time to see the knot of riders pull up in a cloud of dust before the house. Squinting, he tried to make out who they were, but it was only when Larrabee's voice bawled that he recognized the posse for what it was.

"Cullen! We know you're here, mister. Come on outside!"

"Over here, Sheriff," Cullen said tightly. When he went out of the bunkhouse, the four punchers were right back of him and Chin Lee was swearing in a high-pitched voice.

"Keep the hands high!" the sheriff warned, reining across the yard with his gun in his hand. Mayor Garrity was there, too, looking winded and hot, with rotgut seeping from his pores. It was the others who worried

Cullen, the pickup crew of deputies sworn in for this job.

"What are you pulling, Hayes?" Skinner Forbes demanded hotly. "I'm not packing a gun."

"Shut up," Larrabee said, glaring down at the five of them. He jabbed the barrel of the Colt toward the bunkhouse. "Anybody else in there?"

"Yeah. My cook," Cullen said. "Chin, come on out here."

The cook came out still sputtering, but quieted at the sight of guns and the hostile looks from the posse. Cullen told himself he should have expected this, that it was routine and nothing to worry about. But it riled him anyway. It was then he noticed Palmer, the nester who had butchered the X-R cow, and then volunteered to haul Cullen's supplies with Jethro Horn. The man held a shotgun loose under his right arm, and his face was impassive.

"I warned you, Cullen," Larrabee said, and there was satisfaction in the words. "You poked a hornet's nest, and by God it did bust open in your face."

"That's right," Garrity said. "There's been murder done, Cullen, and somebody's going to hang. You can't run over the town this way, no matter how big you are."

Cullen bit down hard enough to keep a profane explosion under his breath. There was little to be gained in that. When he spoke, his tongue was thick with the effort of restraint.

"When you find your man, Hayes, I'll help you hang him. Recollect a bit and you'll remember I've been hollering for law and order a long time. Damn it, you think I'd be fool enough to hire Horn and then gun him down myself? Earl" — he turned to the little man as he spoke — "Tell them where I was all afternoon and evening."

"That's right, Hayes," Wesp said, tension plain in his voice. "The boss was around the place the whole time. I — "

"Hell, you'd lie for him," Garrity said testily. It was plain he was uncomfortable in his present position. "We talked to your wife, Cullen. She told us you didn't do it, and we'll believe her."

"Where *is* Emily?" Cullen said, starting at the mention of his wife. "Is she all right?"

"She's all right," the sheriff broke in. "Wasn't room at the Horn's so she and Marcy stayed at the preacher's. They're safe enough in town; people remember all Emily's done for them. If I was you though, Cullen, I'd think twice before I show myself in Trinidad."

"That's right," Palmer said, his voice self-conscious but firm. "I worked for you to keep mine from starving, but that don't say I can't hate your guts."

"I owe you money, Palmer," Cullen said, remembering it suddenly. He reached for his wallet, but Hayes Larrabee swore at him and thumbed back the hammer of his gun.

"Later, Cullen," he snapped. "Right now we want to know where George Cox is. Palmer here got the idea, and I think it was a good one. Your foreman shot off his mouth pretty big that time you roughed Palmer and his folks up, and we figure he may be the man ambushed Horn."

"The hell!" Cullen spit in the dirt at his feet, but part of his anger stemmed from the jolting thought Larrabee's words brought. Wesp and the others had avoided saying anything about George Cox a while ago.

"I'll talk," Larrabee said roughly, enjoying himself back of the angry mask. "You just answer. Now, where's your fair-haired boy? We can easy beat it out of you."

Cullen stalled. If his foreman had done it, he should pay. But if Cox was innocent, what chance would he have with a posse that would likely settle for any neck, guilty or not? He owed Cox something for the years of loyalty.

"We'll beat it out of you, Cullen," Garrity

echoed, sounding righteously indignant. "And we'll burn your place to find him if he's hiding here. So you better talk, and talk fast."

"George quit me," Cullen said slowly. "He mentioned Wiggins wanting him to come up there."

"If you're lying it'll be rough when we get back," Larrabee told Cullen.

"Hertzog!" Cullen said suddenly. "Can't you see *he* must be the one who did it, Sheriff? He couldn't stand to see me get the best of him, so he hid out and waited for Horn."

"If you didn't put Cox up to the killing," Garrity said, a fat smile loosening his face for the first time since he rode up, "Why are you so anxious to accuse Hertzog? Anyway, Hertzog has a dozen witnesses."

"I didn't know he had that many people working for him," Cullen said angrily. "Why believe him instead of me, Mayor?"

"Because you're about through, Cullen." Garrity snorted, rocking in the saddle as he did. "Hayes told me he warned you when you planned this business. You've pushed us around too long, and now the shoe is on the other foot. You and your man Deems in the Legislature have squeezed the farmer long enough, my friend. You've done your last lording it around here."

"Amen!" Larrabee added. "All right, boys, we ride in five minutes. Meantime, Cullen, you can pay off Palmer here, and I figure you owe the Horn widow some money too."

"I'll take care of that," Cullen said. "Twenty dollars right with you, Palmer?" He got out his wallet, and the red-faced farmer nodded silently.

"Here's twenty-five. I'm very sorry about Jethro Horn." Cullen handed up the money and watched in surprise as Palmer thumbed aside one of the bills and handed it back.

"I'm sorry, too," the farmer said. "But you don't get off for five dollars, Cullen. I don't buy that easy."

The posse watered their horses at the trough, and some of them climbed down to tighten cinches and stretch their legs. When the sheriff bawled, they mounted and rode out in the direction of the Tanks. Chin Lee stamped back into the bunkhouse, jabbering to himself in his own tongue, and Wesp trudged toward the barn. Cullen cursed ineffectually and glared at Skinner Forbes and the two other riders.

"Cob, you and Joe better ride back out to the Tanks and bring the rest of the boys in. I don't know what the crazy bastards in town might do. Skinner, you get out to Twenty Mile and tell Lathrop to forget those strays. Take Wesp along and leave him with the chuck wagon, till this blows over. If George comes back here I don't want tattletale blood on my conscience."

"Right, Boss," Cob Durham said. He licked cracked lips and scuffed dirt with a boot toe. "What about Larrabee and his circus?"

"Dodge them. I don't want anything started by us, understand? This thing can die down as fast as it blew up. I'm going to have a talk with Carl Hertzog pretty soon, and maybe he'll switch tunes."

"Suppose Cox really did it?" Forbes asked.

"He'll hang then," Cullen said. "Get moving, all of you. Just be sure you wait for a real reason before you unlimber a gun. I mean that."

In fifteen minutes they were gone. When they disappeared Cullen went into the bunkhouse and had more coffee while he tried to puzzle the thing out. Chin Lee was still hopping around nervously, and when Cullen told him he'd have to milk the cow in Wesp's absence he threatened to leave.

"Suit yourself," Cullen told him. "It's a long walk to town, though."

Cullen went back to the house and got down the gunbelt from the closet door. Hertzog was heavy on his mind, and he would have ridden to town then except for thinking about George Cox. A combination of guilt and doubt held him in the house, pretending to work at his books, until the clock struck twelve. He went out to the bunkhouse, and Chin Lee fried some ham and potatoes for him.

Cullen had set two o'clock as a deadline, but he wasn't sure what he would have done if the posse hadn't returned half an hour short of that limit. He met them in the yard, and swore aloud when he saw George Cox sitting in the saddle, his arms bound at his sides. One of the nester deputies had a bloody rag knotted about his upper arm, and Cullen held his breath while he counted men. They were all there, eight men wet with sweat and caked with dust, but there was a brassy taste in Cullen's mouth even then.

"Tell them Cullen," Cox said, the words rasping out of lips that were a set slash across his face. The foreman was bareheaded, and there were two raw welts on one cheek and caked blood on his forehead. "Tell them when I pulled out of here on my way to Montana. What a damned fool I was to change my mind and come back!"

"He's right, Hayes," Cullen told the sheriff. No way he could have shot Horn.

"Swear you didn't do it, George," he added, looking intently into his foreman's face. "Tell me that, and I'll see you get off in a hurry."

"Hell! You got a lot of gall sending a posse after *me,* Frank Cullen. A hell of a lot of gall, and I won't forget."

"Watch it, mister," a rider growled. "I'll belt you another one side the head!"

"Don't lie for him, Cullen," Larrabee said. "He tried to kill Jenkins when we caught up to him. You shouldn't of done that, George."

"If I'd wanted to kill him I wouldn't have shot him in the arm, you stupid tinstar!" Cox said. "You had no call to take me, dammit! I hadn't seen a soul until I met your posse!"

"You'll get a trial," the sheriff said. "A damn sight better shake than Horn got, but you'll hang when we're done! Could be you'll even talk enough to put your boss in prison. Come on, boys!" He yanked down the brim of his hat and spurred his horse, purposely running him close enough to make Cullen jump back and shield his face from the dust churning up.

Cox swayed like a drunken man in the saddle, but a rider alongside steadied him with a shove that doubled him forward over the horn. Cullen watched until he lost sight of the posse in the dust and then walked with slow steps to the barn. Uncertainty gnawed inside him and he prayed he hadn't made a mistake. But what choice was there, as positive as he was that Cox was innocent. There was time yet to get in touch with Evan Gentry and have the lawyer defend Cox. But there was little comfort in the knowledge when he remembered the kind of jury that would decide for or against the rope.

He saddled up and rode out of the yard, yelling to the cook that he would be back by dark and then wondering why he bothered to say that. A lot could happen in the hours left him this day. Larrabee had warned against coming to Trinidad, and there was sense to the warning. His first stop would be at the Horn place, and he felt for the wallet in his inside coat pocket. There was a debt to pay, even if young Horn made out the receipt with his shotgun.

The haze of dust fanned out by the posse was barely settling as he rode along the trail. The ranch disappeared below the ridge behind him and Trinidad lay ahead, cooking in the sun. The thought came that Horn's funeral must already have been held in such weather, and he cursed the heat. In a full circle around him the sky was a bowl of shimmering yellow-white that pricked at his eyes like needles. *You hate us, don't you, God?* he asked aloud in a puzzled voice. *You hate every damned one of us!*

CHAPTER 9

Shelly Horn rode home alone from the funeral like a man waking from a dream. What had happened had drained the feeling from him the way this hot sun dried the moisture in him, and he reached the soddy weak and empty. He remembered little of the morning clearly. There had been the dusty ride back of the wagon that carried his father's rough coffin, and the well-meaning, futile attempts of friends to help. Flies had buzzed in the heat, and he could still feel the solidness of the shovel handle in calloused palms as he showered dusty clods down onto the top of the pine box that took his father out of this world. And in the background was the awful crying of his mother.

As he came out of the shade of the barn, a flicker of movement in the distance beyond the road caught at his eyes and he lifted his head to see what it was. Two riders were disappearing beyond a rise, and his forehead creased momentarily as he turned toward the house. Then he remembered the posse and figured these men must be part of it, likely separated from the main force and just now returning to Trinidad.

He tried to savor the taste of justice — of revenge — in his throat, but there was no joy in it. Even hanging Cox wouldn't help. He pushed open the door and crossed the threshold, glad for the dark coolness inside.

The house was much as he had left it. Beds unmade, and the glass of tea Billie Jo had got for Marcy sitting on the table and still three-quarters full. Shelly set to work straightening up, glad Mrs. Palmer had insisted on his mother and sisters staying with her. "Just till Mr. Palmer gets back," the sunburned woman had put it.

Yes, they had all done their best. The reverend had wrung tears from the assembled mourners, tears that soaked quickly into the parched ground underfoot. Marcy Cullen and her mother had been there, not seeming to notice the snubs from the farmers. That cut into Shelly when he remembered all the rancher's wife had done for the church and the town in general. But when Marcy had tried to speak to him he turned away. A week ago he couldn't have believed he'd ever do anything to hurt the girl. When you love someone — the thought made him curse angrily and he broke off. He had been seven kinds of fool to ever dream two people as far apart as he and the daughter of the biggest cattleman around could be anything but enemies.

Will Palmer had been in the jubilant band of riders Shelly had encountered on the way out from town. George Cox, trussed tightly, had sat his saddle and avoided Shelly's eyes as the sheriff boasted how quick he'd been brought to justice. While the others rode for Trinidad, Palmer stayed long enough to tell of Frank Cullen making no effort to aid his foreman. And that he, Palmer, had been paid for his freighting.

"Could have had an extra five," the red-faced man said stiffly. "But I didn't want any part of the strings with it. Don't reckon I have to tell you not to take bribe money, Shelly."

The thought of the money came back to Shelly as he sank tiredly onto his cot and pulled off his shoes. There was pay owed to the Horns from Cullen. It would help, but somehow there had to be more if Shelly was to do the thing that was shaping itself in his mind.

He was the head of the house now, with his widowed mother and his sisters his responsibility. Likely what he had decided would hurt his father, if there was any hereafter. All the work meaningless, all the sacrifices for nothing but admission of failure. Yet what other answer was there but to send the womenfolk back home?

Fatigue must have made him doze, because when he heard the noise of a rider approaching it was near dark. Still slow with sleep, he swung his feet onto the floor and pushed erect. For some reason he didn't understand, he went for the shotgun leaned in the corner. When he opened the door, Frank Cullen was swinging down from his mount a dozen yards away. A tightness paralyzed Shelly's chest muscles to the point where breathing was hard.

"It's me, Frank Cullen," the rancher said stiffly, hiking at the gunbelt that looked odd on him. He squinted at the house in the gathering dark and spoke again. "That you, Shelly Horn?"

"You're right." Shelly moved into the yard, vowing not to ask the rancher into the house the way his pa would have done.

"You'd rather I take the gun off?" Cullen asked, eyeing the shotgun gripped in Shelly's hands. "I came to pay you the wages coming to your father."

"You can leave the money on the stoop, I reckon." Shelly said, wetting his lips and knowing he must look foolish holding to the shotgun. Something told him he had little to fear from the rancher, that whatever else the man might be, he wouldn't do anything as crude as cutting him down in his own yard. Cullen didn't have to do that anyway.

"Twenty dollars was the agreement," Cullen said, drawing some bills from his pocket. He took a tentative step toward Shelly, as though to hand him the money. Then, as the boy moved aside, gesturing with the barrel of the shotgun, he shrugged slightly and set down the money Jethro Horn had earned with his life.

"I'm sorry, son," Cullen said awkwardly. "I hope you believe that."

"I'm sorry, too," Shelly flung back bitterly. "I missed you at the funeral, Mr. Cullen. But I guess you got more important work to take care of."

"About that — " The rancher broke off, began again, "I plan to take care of the expenses. Not that I take responsibility for the shooting, but — "

"Save your breath. It's taken care of already. Len Hicks don't have much money, but he built the coffin. The reverend didn't charge, either. And the land Pa's takin' up now didn't cost much. Like you said, twenty dollars squares us."

"All right, damn it," Cullen flared, and Shelly could see his drawn face clearly. Then the rancher caught himself, sighing heavily. "Your mother — is there any money to — ?"

"We don't need charity from you, Mr. Cullen," Shelly said evenly. "Ma and the girls are over to town for a while. I'll look out for things. Likely they'll go back home when I got the money to send them."

"Oh." Cullen tried to hide his pleasure at the news, but Shelly caught it. "Sorry things didn't work out for you folks, but I've said all along this is no place for farmers."

"I know. You preached it like religion. Ma believes it now. I almost did, but not quite. I didn't say *I* was going back."

"The funeral," Cullen said after a gap of silence. "My wife — she was there?"

"Mrs. Cullen was there," Shelly told him. "Marcy was too. I'm indebted to both of them. Your wife is a good Christian woman."

"Whose money built that precious church?" Cullen demanded, and Shelly could hear breath whistle from his nostrils. "Who — oh hell, what's the use. My daughter, Horn. What is she to you?"

The new tack caught Shelly off guard, and he stammered foolishly before he could get his tongue under control. He wasn't sure himself just what the rancher's daughter was to him — now.

"I planned once to marry Marcy," he said

defiantly at last. The sweat in his hands told him he was gripping the shotgun too tightly. "Even that time you treated me like dirt in town — "

"Maybe *especially* then, son?" Cullen coaxed. "You aimed to get even, take me down a peg. That was it, wasn't it? Not love for Marcy, but a kind of revenge."

"You wanted her to marry your foreman," Shelly retorted, half-guiltily. Cullen's accusation roused worrying shadows of doubt in his mind. "Her kind — a rancher. You still proud of George Cox?"

"I face facts, Horn. This is ranch country, and I've given most of my life to it. Before you were born, almost, I was fighting the toughness and the dryness. It was what I believed in, what I knew. You think I wanted to see the only child I had marry a farmer, a sworn enemy who came in on a politician's coattails to do me out of what cost me twenty years?"

"I don't give a damn *what* you wanted, Cullen," Shelly said, so soft he could barely hear his voice himself. "And all I want now is justice for my father's murder. After that — I'll worry about the rest later."

"If George Cox killed your father, I want to see him hanged," Cullen said, in a voice that jarred Shelly for its sincerity. "But I'm not yet convinced he did it. In the first place, why would he commit murder? A man with a future — "

"Maybe he was *guaranteeing* that future," Shelly said harshly. It was dark now, and he couldn't see the rancher except in vague outline. "Driving out us farmers meant a lot to you. Cox would have been a fool not to have done your bidding with a stake like that. The X-R — and Marcy too."

"If I wanted a man killed I'd do the job myself," Cullen said bluntly. "I don't have to hire another man's gun, and the day I do I'll ride out of this country and not come back."

"You talk big for someone who doesn't mind buying representation for himself in Austin," Shelly said hotly. "Everybody knows why Deems is beholden to you."

"All right, Horn, let's call a spade a spade," the rancher retorted. "Deny, if you can, that the nesters are buying that same representation with votes, and then tell me who's less honest! I've told you what I have in X-R, and if you think I'll stand by like a fool and watch my land stolen from me you're crazier than most. Of course, I contribute to Deems. If I didn't I'd have gone under by now."

"We want nothing of yours," Shelly protested. "Just our rights, and a chance — "

"*Your* rights? Was Palmer in his rights when he cut my fence and butchered my beef? Is it right that my taxes be used for relief for you farmers who failed just like I warned you would? I was wrong when I gave for the church and the school in Trinidad. My own daughter went to school in the East, so I was putting little nesters through the grades with money better spent shipping them back where they belonged!"

"I'll give you credit," Shelly said grudgingly. "You never pretended otherwise, Cullen. But being honest doesn't make a man right. If Cox didn't shoot my father, who did?"

"Hertzog," Cullen answered without hesitation. "It galled him that I'd beat him at his own game, and all he could think to do was put me in a bad light this way."

"Like you hoped he would?" Shelly asked accusingly. "Can you deny that, since we're baring our souls? There are no witnesses, so it's just my word against yours."

"That makes me think you don't believe Cox did it," Cullen said, almost triumphantly. "That and one other thing. Any man facing someone he thought killed his own flesh and blood would do more than let the killer pass on. Likely the posse would have given you a gun to do the job and then made a story to cover it. Either you don't think Cox was the killer or else you're a yellow coward."

"We're wasting time," Shelly said, irritated by the sore spot the rancher had just rubbed. When he watched his father die, hadn't he said that all he wanted was the shotgun and revenge? Seeing Cox, he had felt no such killing hate. *Was* he weak, pushing off his responsibility to other men acting under the respectability of the law?

"You're right," Cullen said. "We *are* wasting time." He straightened, and the sound of creaking leather at his waist came to Shelly. "I came to settle with you, and I have, as far as your stiffnecked pride would let me. Now I'm going to ride into town and arrange for a lawyer for George Cox before the lynchers can take over."

"That was no lynch mob," Shelly said, as much to himself as to Cullen. "The sheriff deputized those men legally. The mayor was along, too."

"Garrity?" Cullen said harshly. "He's got to do *something* for his pay. Your legality is mighty one-sided, Horn, if you'll stop and consider. All depends on whose ox is being gored."

"You offered charity," Shelly said, changing the subject abruptly, "and I refused. I'll *work* for you, though. Like I told you, I need money to send Ma and the girls home."

"Work for me?" Plainly it jarred Cullen. "What could you do on a ranch, besides maybe muck out the barn?"

"I can drive a team," Shelly said, keeping his voice under control. "Hertzog won't be apt to haul for you now any more than he would before. I'll take the job at the same rate you paid Pa."

"You mean — you'd hire on, knowing what happened to your father?"

"That's right," Shelly said. "You should jump at the chance, too. That way you might get rid of an unwanted suitor for Marcy. And your hands would be even cleaner this time because I know for sure what I'm going into. How about it?"

"You're serious." It was a statement uttered in disbelief. "I think you'd really do it, Shelly, and I'm a fool for not taking you up on it. But I won't. I'll give you the money for all of you to go back to where you came from, but the blame for one man's death is enough."

"I don't need pity," Shelly said. "If you want, I'll sign a paper releasing you from any responsibility."

"We're wasting time, but I — admire you, damned if I don't. Or maybe I *should* pity you. Forget what I said about being yellow, I was wrong."

"Thanks for the twenty dollars," Shelly said, sure now that Cullen was done talking. "It'll help, and I'll raise the rest somehow. I'll be staying, though, and you've got no promise as far as Marcy is concerned."

"Neither have you," Cullen snapped. "I told you I'm going to see George Cox has a fair shake on this thing. Marcy may see reason yet."

"Fair enough. I won't be part of a lynch mob if your foreman doesn't get a decent trial. Goodby, Mr. Cullen."

"Goodby," the rancher said. He turned away, and a moment later there came the creak of saddle leather as he pulled himself up. "My sympathies about your father. And I'll see that the killer pays for it."

Shelly leaned against the side of the soddy, relaxing his grip on the shotgun at last. He was sure he still hated this high and mighty rancher, and yet there was an odd respect for the man now. In spite of Cullen's seeming confidence and hardness, Shelly was aware of something pathetic too. Twenty years of fighting this cruel land, the rancher had said. And his remark about the farmers buying with votes what Cullen had to pay for in cash had an element of truth in it.

The dull clumping of hooves in the dust

told him the rancher was out to the road now, turning toward town. Shelly reached down, feeling on the worn steps for the money that was Jethro Horn's debt. He straightened and folded the bills, feeling hunger pangs in his stomach for the first time that day. It had been a long time since Marcy had brought him coffee and biscuits and made him eat. There would be something in the cupboard, and he could make coffee. Wearily he pushed open the door, just as the crash of a handgun shattered the dark quiet of the hot night.

The sound of it shook him so that he wasn't sure of what happened next. Vaguely he heard Cullen's pained curse echoing in the lull of quiet between the gun blast and the echoes back from the foothills. Shelly got the door open again, then tripped, sprawling in the dirt outside the soddy. On hands and knees he heard Cullen's strained voice shouting his name.

"Damn you, Shelly Horn! You were pretty smart with that smooth, noble talk. I didn't think you'd gun me down — especially from behind!"

"Cullen, wait!" Shelly shouted the words in confusion. He had no idea what had happened, but the wild thought came that the rancher might be mortally hit and would die thinking Shelly had pulled the trigger of a coward's gun!

"You'll regret just winging me, you young fool," Cullen called out viciously.

"I didn't shoot!" Shelly cried, and realization that he was empty-handed made him scramble for the door and search in the dark for the shotgun.

As he came back out, another shot tore apart the quiet, and he heard the ricochet, and the rattle of sand on fenceposts. For part of a second he was afraid the shot had finished Cullen, that the ambusher in the dark had succeeded. Then the rancher swore.

"Get back in the house, farmer boy!" another voice yelled. "Keep out of this and you won't get hurt! This is — " A third shot drowned the rest, a shot that must have come from Cullen's gun.

In answer, flame showed off to the left as a second bushwhacker fired at the telltale flash from Cullen's gun. Cullen was caught in a crossfire, doomed to die — if he wasn't already dead. Emotions tore at Shelly. If vigilantes wanted to take matters in hand, why should he risk his neck? All he had to do was obey. Go back in the house and keep his nose clean. Instead, he lifted the shotgun to his shoulder and fired in the direction, as best as he could remember, of the last gun flash.

CHAPTER 10

The shotgun tore a ragged hole in the brief quiet, slamming back against his shoulder enough to make Shelly wince. He had little chance of doing any good at this distance. Like strung firecrackers came two more shots, the thinner, slapping noise of handguns. In the darkness, it was more a dream than a real gunfight, and it wasn't until splinters of wood from the door in back of him stung his neck that Shelly dove for the dirt in the yard.

Spitting sand and trying to reason whether or not he was hit or just scared, he heard an agonized cry that choked off and was followed by a dull, thudding sound. When a voice cried out exultantly, Shelly was strangely relieved that it was Cullen and not one of his ambushers.

"That's one!" the rancher bawled hoarsely. "Thanks, Horn, I misjudged you. Stay covered, boy!"

For a split second, Shelly had thought his shotgun blast had hit home, that the cry came from a man struck by his load. Now with the knowledge that it was Cullen who hit the mark came a wash of relief. Shelly had hunted all his life; the gun he held now had brought down birds and killed small game to put meat on the table. He had fired a rifle at antelope when he could borrow one and could afford cartridges, which wasn't often. But he'd never fired at a man.

Shelly was shaking now, and his stomach writhed in spite of its emptiness so that he thought he was going to vomit right there in the dirt. He couldn't understand why he had rushed forward into the dark to aid a man he still held accountable for the death of his father, a man who stood for all the things Jethro Horn hadn't believed in. Now, flat on the ground, he realized he might have killed a man he didn't even know. He could be killed himself, now that he had made his play and chosen a side in an ambush that could have rid him of Frank Cullen once and for all. Afraid to breathe, he wondered how it would feel to catch a bullet.

"You played it wrong," a voice shouted in front of him and to the left. "I told you this wasn't your squabble, son. Hell, you ought to be glad to get rid of Cullen. He killed your old man, didn't he?"

"Keep talking, Hertzog," Cullen said, his voice lower now and strangely calm. "You're next, once I know just where to shoot."

The freighter's curse was blotted out by the crash of his gun. Shelly, watching closely, saw no telltale flame but heard the wet, heavy *thuck* as the slug hit something. He hadn't recognized the ambusher's voice until Cullen pointed it out, but it was Carl Hertzog all right. And Cullen had said it was the freighter who killed Jethro Horn!

"Keep shooting," Cullen said, still calm. "My horse can't feel anything now, and sooner or later I'll pinpoint you. Fenceposts aren't much cover."

Shelly had wondered how the rancher was still alive; knowing about the barricade cleared that up. Cullen's mount must have been killed by one of the shots, or maybe Cullen had shot it intentionally for cover. Shelly tried to picture the situation in his mind. Cullen was on the road, he was sure of that much. To the right of the dead horse, now that the gunman on that side seemed finished off.

Hertzog and his companion must have come through the old pasture across the road, crouching back of the posts that were tied together raggedly with strands of barbed wire. Unless the freighter had more men staked out somewhere in the darkness, the gun battle could become a Mexican stand-off. The moon would be late, Shelly remembered, and he licked his dirt-caked lips and prayed that Hertzog would crawl back to where he had left his own horse and clear out.

"I'm not worried about you, Cullen," Hertzog said after the empty pause. "That first shot hit you — likely you're dying now. It's Horn I'm concerned about. Kid, you get on back in the house, understand? After a while you can come out and find Cullen's body. Nobody knows who did it, nobody cares."

"He's got a point, Shelly," Cullen said bitterly. "Only he forgot to tell you, you'll get the blame for killing me. After all, you've got plenty reason to want to."

"He's only got a shotgun, Cullen! No six-shooter, see?" Hertzog called. "Besides, Horn, suppose you are suspected of killing him. Who'd blame you for that? They'd credit you, instead. Use your head, boy. You've had enough grief for a while."

"Why did you shoot his father, Hertzog?" Cullen bellowed. "Because you hated his guts for taking the job? Or was it to get me in bad with the boy, and the law, and the whole town?"

"Hell, who says I shot the old man?" Hertzog yelled angrily. "Your own foreman will hang for that, Cullen, and you know it. You knew that, didn't you, Horn? George Cox,

Cullen's right hand, Horn. And his pay was to be Cullen's daughter, wasn't that the deal, Cullen?"

"If it's true, what are you doing out here skulking around in the dark trying to shoot me in the back?" Cullen answered. "You thought you had me over a barrel, Hertzog. That you could squeeze me for more money because I was in a bind. When I found a way out you couldn't stand it, could you?"

"Go to hell!" Hertzog shouted. "You're lying in your teeth, the way your kind has always done."

"Just one thing bothers me," Cullen said evenly. "Aren't you killing the golden goose, Hertzog? Where do you figure to make your money freighting?"

"By God, you do rate yourself high, don't you?" came the answer. "You're through, Cullen, even if you're the only one can't see it. Too bad you can't live to be broken the way the town plans to break you, you conceited bastard! Treat people like dirt, and think they have to take it because you've got the money to pay."

"You don't make sense," Cullen said. "A man like you don't suddenly get religion, Hertzog. It's not principle, but fear for your rotten hide that brought you out here to cut me down."

"If you'd played it smart you could have lived, big man," Hertzog yelled, his voice shrill. "But you had to tell the law it was me done it, Cullen. Damned if Larrabee didn't come nosing into my place today, asking questions like he thought I *did* have a hand in it."

"You can quit squealing now," Cullen said. "Shelly, I'm afraid you're in a tight spot, and believe me, I'm sorry for that. You can go on inside, and if he does finish me off you'll have that satisfaction. But you'll live with the rest of it, too, boy. You'll know the man that killed your father murdered another innocent man under your nose. Maybe you'll even get the blame — or the credit — for that."

"Shut up, Cullen, damn you!" Shelly cried. "Shut up before — "

"It's a tough choice, son. If you stay out here you may end up alongside your father while the dirt's still fresh over him. I thank you for what you did for me, and I'm done talking. It's your play, Shelly. And — God help you, boy." In the silence after Cullen got done talking there was only the sound of a six-gun cylinder rotating.

All his life Shelly Horn had been taught not to kill. Violence and death were alien to him, and fear was akin to sickness as he got to his knees. The stock of the shotgun dragged audibly on the still warm ground, and he sucked in his breath and froze rigid. When the shot he feared didn't come, he could think again. He tried to think right.

It was all in the Bible, his pa had told him every time he was faced with a decision. But the Bible was a thick book and hard to read. He tried to remember, to make passages fit. *Thou shalt not kill* came to him, drumming through his mind. And *Honor thy father and thy mother*. He tried desperately to hold to all he had been taught, all his parents believed and tried to teach him. When he was done thinking, it was simply a choice. A choice between what was right and what was wrong. As quietly as he could, he stood up and began moving in a crouch toward the barn.

Five, ten, fifteen soft, slow steps. He reached the heavier darkness alongside the lean-to, and it was still quiet. Licking his lips, he worked his mouth to coax moisture back into it so that he could speak.

"Carl Hertzog? You hearing this?"

"I hear you, son. Play it smart now." There was a rustle of sound across the road.

"I want you to move off my place, Hertzog. There'll be no more killing here tonight. You, Cullen. Hold your fire, or I'll have to shoot you. I think I can do it from here, and I have one barrel still loaded in this scattergun."

"You damned fool! You crazy damned fool!" It was Hertzog, and now Shelly knew he was lying back of the thick post two or three down from where the path from the house turned into the road. A cottonwood stump, and one of the few sizable enough to hide a man.

"I mean it, Hertzog. You move out, now, or I'm coming for you. I know where you are."

"I warned you enough," Hertzog yelled. "You haven't got a chance in hell with that shotgun, Horn. Don't try to be a hero!"

"I'm coming, then." On shaking legs, Shelly left the lee of the barn and began moving down the ruts toward the road. He cradled the gun in stiff hands, hands that felt suddenly huge and puffy. He was a fool, like Hertzog said, or a lunatic. Both, likely.

It was dark enough that he couldn't make out the post the freighter must be hidden behind. But Hertzog must not be able to see him either. Shelly knew each hump and hollow of the ground, setting his feet down with desperate care. He reached the road itself, and no shot had cut him down.

"Pull out, Hertzog," he said, straining his

eyes to see. "You've still got time."

"I'll kill you both!" Hertzog flung back at him. "Just a little closer is all I ask, you fool!"

"Go on back, son," Cullen called. It was twice the rancher had called him son now and it rankled Shelly without his knowing why. "Go back and we'll wait him out. There'll be a moon in an hour or so."

"Only you won't be alive to see it!" Hertzog shouted. "Neither of you will. Come on, Horn. Come and get it!"

The horse in the barn moved, bumping the stall, and Shelly gritted his teeth with the noise. There was a faint clicking that might have been Hertzog's gun or Cullen's, he wasn't sure which.

"I was baiting you," Cullen said sharply, an edge of concern in his voice that was new. "Get back to the house before you get a bullet in the belly."

"Rather that than in the back," Shelly said grimly, and edged forward. There was no turning aside now, he was sure. Cullen had spelled it out for him clear enough a moment ago, and if that hadn't been enough, Hertzog had finished it. This thing was for settling now, whichever way it went. He had a chance, slim as it was. Shelly had figured it out as best he could; the rest was up to God.

"I can see you now," he lied. The cottonwood post was barely discernible in the darkness, but maybe Hertzog would believe him. "One more chance, Hertzog. Clear out, or I'll let you have this load of buckshot."

"You're bluffing," Hertzog said, laughing as he called the bluff. There was one thing left, and Shelly did that. He pulled the second trigger on the shotgun and threw himself sidewise even as the butt dug into his shoulder.

Belatedly he saw the freighter, etched by the blue flame from his gun barrel as he knelt alongside the post. Lying in the dirt for the second time in this nightmare that had started so long ago, Shelly thought he had heard two shots and wondered how Hertzog triggered them off so fast. It wasn't until he heard the low moaning curse and the sound of the freighter falling that he knew the second shot had been Cullen's. His gamble had paid off!

"Don't move a muscle, Shelly, he may be playing possum!" the rancher called from his barricade. "That was good thinking, son. Damned good thinking!"

For maybe two minutes there was only the hoarse gasping of Hertzog, and Shelly lay, expecting another shot to probe for him any second. Then a short, satisfied grunt jarred him, and he raised his head in surprise.

"All right, son, I just booted this possum's gun far enough away he won't find it tonight. Go get a lantern and we'll see how bad he's hurt."

Still clutching the empty shotgun, Shelly scrambled up and moved toward the post. He could see Cullen as the rancher holstered his six-gun and stood looking down at the man who had tried to kill him.

"You're not hurt?" Shelly asked in surprise.

"My shoulder's half-killing me," Cullen said with a short laugh. "But I think maybe I'll live. Will you go get a light?"

"Sure I will," Shelly said, turning away. It was over now, and there was time to think about what he had done. To wonder if he had planned any of it, or just acted on blind, despairing impulse. As he passed the barn he reeled on weak legs like a drunken man and caught at the rough boards for support. The shotgun slid from his hand and his stomach churned. When he was through vomiting he went the rest of the way to the house, choking down shame along with the sour taste that clung in his mouth.

By the time he found the lantern, lit it, and returned, Cullen was knotting his bandanna around his left arm with his right hand and his teeth. The glow of the lantern caught the set, hard planes of the rancher's face and the drops of sweat that beaded his forehead. Apparently he had lost his hat at the outset, and the grayness of his hair glinted in the light.

"I'm all right," Cullen said, squeezing at the bandage. "But I wouldn't bet on Hertzog." He nodded at the freighter, leaning back against the post, both arms wrapped about his middle.

"Not much blood, but it's bad in the guts. We've got to get him to town if you have a wagon on the place," Cullen decided.

"I'll hitch up," Shelly said. "How about the other one?"

"That was Henry Lang," Cullen told him, shaking his head. "We can leave him off at the cemetery. Shelly?"

"What?" Shelly turned back at his name, to see Cullen reaching a hand toward him.

"Thanks," the rancher said. "I don't know that I deserved your help, but — "

"Forget it," Shelly said, almost angrily. He ignored the outstretched hand. "You said it yourself — I had no choice."

He turned away, but the hurt look on the rancher's face stayed with him. There was nothing owing Cullen, even now. The man's seeming concern for getting Hertzog to town

162

wasn't because of the wound so much as the testimony the freighter would give to clear Cullen. Nothing had changed, and there was no cause for Shelly to feel different. But he realized guiltily that he had never really believed that Cullen could have killed his father.

The moon was a slanted crescent over the foothills as they drove toward Trinidad. Shelly pushed the old horse as much as he could, but the animal was still worn from the toll of the last few days. Cullen hunched patiently on the seat beside him, and in the bed of the wagon lay one dead man and another likely dying. A hearse, Shelly thought bitterly, but now he was almost too tired to pursue the idea. If this was an end to it, he would take that and be grateful.

Trinidad was quieter than he expected, though when he thought of it there was no reason for it to be otherwise. He reined up at the jail, watching Cullen drop from the seat and hurry inside, yelling for Larrabee. Someone swore and told him the sheriff was home, then a swamper came out to look in the wagon and the quiet was broken.

By the time Shelly had come back to the jail with the doctor, it looked like half the town was trying to crowd into the small building. There were plenty of witnesses to hear the freighter's halting admission of guilt and listen to his story of the ambush that backfired.

"By damn!" Larrabee exploded. "If this don't put a different face on the picture! We got no call to hold Cox now, I reckon."

"Let's string up Hertzog instead!" someone bawled. "Fetch a rope, and we'll do it now!"

"You're comin' along, eh, Shelly?" someone shouted in his ear. "I reckon you got more right than anybody else in this town!"

Before Shelly had time to think, the doctor stood up and waved his arms.

"Shut up, you pack of fools!" he commanded. "Just wait a day or two and you won't have to lynch him. Intestines don't mend easy. Frank, you better sit down and let me take a look at that shoulder of yours."

"Later," Cullen said impatiently. "I got something more important to do now, Doc. Shelly, this concerns you directly. Come with me over to the depot."

Too tired to protest that he wanted no charity even now, Shelly moved to follow Cullen out of the grumbling, hooting mob. At least this was an escape from the noise and the stink of sweat. As they passed the jail he made out the face of George Cox, framed between the bars of a cell. The foreman would be set free now. That was what Shelly had accomplished by walking straight into Hertzog's gun! He went into the depot behind Cullen, finally protesting against what he supposed the rancher was planning.

"I told you I didn't want your charity, Cullen," he said stiffly. "Now I'd better get back out to the place — "

"Don't holler before you're hurt," Cullen said, and his mouth curled into a tight grin. "I'm not buying transportation for your womenfolk. I'm sending a wire I thought you might be interested in."

Puzzled, Shelly watched him wet the stump of pencil the agent gave him and bend over the counter to write. A minute later Cullen handed the sheet of paper to the agent and told him to read it back so there wouldn't be any mistake.

"Congressman J.R. Deems, State Capitol, Austin, Texas. Advise you back move for farm relief. Letter follows. Signed, Frank Cullen."

"All right, Leggett," Cullen said, nodding. He swung around to face Shelly, still grinning. "I guess there's no fool like an old fool, son. What do you think?"

Before Shelly could answer, a harsh voice did it for him. He turned to the doorway to see George Cox framed in it, his face

165

twisted in hate.

"I think you said it right, Cullen," the man said. "There's no fool like an old fool."

CHAPTER 11

For ten seconds there was no sound in the depot except for the ticking of the clock on the wall above Shelly's head. Then Cox laughed without softening the expression on his face. In the lamplight an angry wound at the side of his forehead showed dark under his hat, but it was the man's eyes that held Shelly and put prickles of fear in his belly.

"Hello, George," Cullen said lamely. He turned until his back was full to the low rail and braced his hands on it. "I told you you wouldn't stay in jail."

"Keep working on that," Cox said, moving across the planked floor slowly, boot heels thudding with each step. "You sure need something to square things now."

Cullen waited for his ex-foreman to come to a halt before him, and Shelly could watch the slow intake and expulsion of breath as it tautened and then creased the rancher's shirt. Cullen gave no sign that he was afraid of Cox, in spite of the deadly look in the man's eyes. Perhaps because of the two guns slung from his waist.

"It was Hertzog, like I figured," Cullen said finally. "He'll hang for it now, unless he dies first. His man Henry Lang is dead, too. I'm sorry for what happened to you, George, but you should have kept on to Montana."

"Sorry, hell!" Cox said. He laughed again, shorter and tighter this time. "This is what I get for my three years, eh, Cullen? You're giving up to these snotnoses." He jerked his head toward Shelly without taking his eyes from Cullen's.

"I'm not giving up to anybody," Cullen said. He sounded tired, and Shelly thought suddenly of the wound in the rancher's shoulder. "We all of us make mistakes, George. I'm trying to even up for one of mine."

"That's what happens to a man when he lives with two women," Cox said. "They got to you, didn't they? Now you're going to lie down with the lambs like mealymouth over there."

"Shelly saved my life tonight. He could have looked the other way — he had every right to. Like I said, a man makes mistakes."

"Yeah. I made one for three years, Cullen, ever thinking you really had the guts to whip these hayshakers. So now you're grooming this one for your daughter's bed. Or maybe he beat you to it and you've got no choice?"

Shelly felt himself color, and his lips flat-
tened as his teeth ground together. Confused
emotions tore at him, but he stayed where
he was, surprised at the tight balling of fists
that happened without his volition.

"That's enough, George," Cullen said
coldly. "I'm sorry the way things worked
out, but don't push me, because I won't
take it."

"Push *you?*" Cox half turned and looked
toward Shelly as if to draw him in as witness.
"I bust my tail for you and you turn me
over to a lynch mob without an aye, no,
or kiss-my-behind, and now you talk about
me pushing *you?* By God, I'm going to do
it at that!"

"We can talk this out," Cullen said, but
it was evident he was close to breaking.
Back of him, Leggett watched open-mouthed,
eyes peering out between the top of his thick
glasses and the green shade he wore. "Come
on over to Gilliam's, George," Cullen added.
"We'll figure where we stand."

"I know where *I* stand, mister. And I'm
beginning to know about you." Cox's voice
had suddenly gone flat and almost resigned,
so the vicious jab of his right arm came as
more of a surprise.

Shelly heard the blow land in Cullen's middle and heard the grunt of pain. As the

rancher's arms dropped, Cox smashed his left hand across Cullen's face, straightened quickly and yanked both guns from Cullen's holsters as he sagged onto the floor.

"You watching, Horn?" Cox demanded with savage triumph. "When I get finished with my old boss you're next. Get on your feet, Cullen."

Sick at his stomach, Shelly watched Cox put the guns on the counter. Then he turned and stumbled for the door, sucking in air as he ran. The knowledge that he was a coward was numb misery, but there was no point in heroics. Alone he would be no help to Cullen against the foreman who had gone mad. As he crossed the road, he yelled hoarsely for Hayes Larrabee.

There were still a few halfhearted hangers-on at the doorway to the jail, but he pushed through them and shouted Larrabee's name again. The beefy sheriff got up irritably from back of his desk.

"Damn it. You reckon I'll get this report done tonight, Clay? What the hell do you want, Horn?"

"You better get over to the depot before Cox kills Cullen!" Shelly said in a rush of words. "Come on!"

"Cox ain't even got a gun," the deputy, Clay, protested. "And Cullen was armed when he went out of here."

"Cox hit him and took the guns," Shelly said, ashamed of himself. "You coming, or you want more killing tonight?"

"If you want to know, Horn, I'd as soon them two killed each other, yes. But I reckon I got to stop it. Clay, you see them fools don't get back in here and bother Hertzog, understand? Come on, kid."

With Larrabee at his back, Shelly pushed into the depot just as he heard the sound of wood splintering. Inside, he saw Cullen push to his hands and knees in the shamble of the railing. Leggett was cursing thinly, still holding to the message Cullen had given him a few minutes before.

"Get up, you son of a bitch," Cox taunted. "And I'll break some more ribs for you."

"Hold it up, Cox," Hayes Larrabee said. "Leave Cullen be."

"Sure," the man said. "Soon as he admits he's bred his girl to a snotnose cottonpicker to raise more of the same. That right, Cullen?"

Cullen swayed erect now, wiping blood awkwardly from his mouth with his right hand as he favored the injured shoulder. With the other hand he motioned Larrabee back, mumbling something Shelly couldn't make out. Gamely the rancher closed with Cox, flailing desperately when he was in range.

With a snort, Cox took the blow on his forearm. Overconfident, he paused momentarily without making any effort to guard against the next wild swing. Cullen's fist landed on the side of Cox's face, a glancing blow but enough to draw a curse from the younger man.

While the sheriff hesitated, Cox doubled his left fist and rammed it into Cullen's middle. As the rancher clutched himself in pain and fell forward, Cox clubbed down mightily with his open right hand, taking the rancher in the back of the neck and driving him to the floor. This time Cullen made no effort to get up. Hayes Larrabee swore under his breath.

"You had your fun now, Cox," he said. "How about if you ride on out of town without no more trouble, eh?"

"Don't worry, Larrabee," Cox told him, spitting on his knuckles and wiping blood from them. "I tried to tell you I was leaving the country when you jumped me, so don't get so goddam edgy now."

"Watch your mouth," the sheriff said, dropping his hands to his gun butts. "I'll throw you back in the same cell for disturbing the peace if you get hard with me."

"Hell, you ought to give me a medal for working Cullen over," Cox said, laughing.

"He's no hero to anybody in Trinidad. One more piece of unfinished business, and then I'll ride north out of this stinking place. Come on, Horn. You were man enough to get to Cullen's daughter. Let's see how you bleed."

"Cox, maybe you think you're tough, and maybe you are," Larrabee said. "Now that I think a minute on it, you got a rough deal when we figured you was the one plugged Jethro Horn. So I'll forget what you did to Cullen. Just come on down to the stable, and I'll get your horse out of hock so you can take off for Montana."

"You going to hide back of him, eh Horn?" Cox taunted. "Cullen can really pick them, can't he? A yellow-belly for a son-in-law!"

Shelly swallowed hard. He kept his eyes tight on Cox, sure the man would make a break toward him at any second, and his skin crawled with the thought of big fists smashing at him. The slight movement at the corner of his eye was Cullen, arching his back in an effort to get his knees up under him again.

"Daddy! Oh, Daddy!" The girl's words swiveled every head toward the doorway, and Shelly watched as Marcy Cullen moved quickly into the light. For a second she held a hand to her mouth as though to stifle a cry, and then she was on her knees in the

173

dust and dirt. Gently she cradled her father's head in her lap, patting his face as though to smooth away the blood and the pain.

"What have they done to you, Daddy?" she half whispered, half wept.

"He had it coming," Cox said harshly. "Your old man got off easy after the way he threw me to that lynch mob."

"Did you have to stand there and let him do this?" Marcy asked suddenly, her eyes accusing Shelly and Larrabee. "They told me he was shot, and now this — " She started to cry as Leggett limped around the counter with an enamel basin half-filled with water and a dingy piece of toweling. Tenderly Marcy began to sponge away the blood from Cullen's face.

"Your farm boy didn't have the guts even to stay and watch, Marcy," Cox said, his eyes fixed on the girl as she bent over her father. "Farmer Horn ran outside for the law!"

"You — animal!" Marcy said, without looking up. "You're not fit to live, George Cox."

"You're going to regret the choice you made. Damn little fool — had a man once and put him off for this lintback."

Marcy looked up, color rising into her face. Then she bit her lip and wrung out the cloth again.

"Get out, Cox," Larrabee said. "You've made enough trouble for one night."

"Sure," Cox shrugged as though it suddenly was of no importance to him. He half turned away, and then whirled back quickly. While Shelly watched helplessly, and before the sheriff could do anything, Cox had dragged Marcy up from the floor beside her father and stumbled back to the counter. With a quick movement of his free hand he grabbed one of Cullen's guns and shoved it into his belt. The other he leveled at Larrabee.

"I told you I had business with Shelly Horn yet," Cox said evenly. "Sheriff, I got nothing special against you anymore. This is private between Horn and me, so you keep out of it and you won't get hurt."

"By God, Cox, we'll have to hang you yet! If you hurt that girl — "

"Hurt her?" Cox laughed. "I wouldn't touch her, Larrabee, except I need a shield for a minute."

There was an excited jabbering of voices outside, and Shelly shifted his eyes long enough to see the mayor in the crowd back of Larrabee in the doorway. But there was little relief in that.

"Horn, I know you're too chicken-livered to fight me with your hands, so I don't expect that satisfaction. In fact, I know you're too

175

yellow to fight unless you've got all the odds."

"Shelly — " Marcy cried, but Cox tightened his arm across the girl's waist, cutting off her breath. She twisted in pain and struggled helplessly to free herself. Shelly stood stock-still and hated himself. But something kept him from charging across the depot to the girl's aid.

With his thumb Cox rotated the cylinder of the gun in his hand. Nodding his satisfaction, he shifted it to his left hand and dug the second gun from his belt. Then, with no warning, he tossed it straight at Shelly. Larrabee swore in a shocked voice as Shelly caught the handgun.

"You got five shots in there, Horn," Cox said. "I got one in this one. That fair enough? All you got to do is pull the trigger, and that don't take much guts. Five to one, and I'll let you shoot first."

"I'll — go with you — " Marcy gasped, trying to twist enough to face Cox. "George, don't — "

"Shut up!" Cox snapped. "You think I'd have a farmer's leavings? How about it, Horn? My left hand, your right."

"Cox, don't be a damn fool," Larrabee broke in. He was holding his own guns as helplessly as though they were broken-off plough handles. "You've had your fun —

you've proved your point. Horn ain't going to fight you, fists, guns, or horsewhips. That right, boy?"

Shelly licked at his lips, still holding the gun in both his hands. He could feel the cartridges in the cylinder; Cox hadn't been lying about that much of it.

"I said how about it, Horn? You say the word, and everybody but you and me clear out of this place. You can't miss with five shots, can you? We've got a showdown coming, and you won't get those odds next time. How about it?"

"Cox, you're crazy. There's a dozen men outside, and you can't get away with it. Don't be a fool." It was Mayor Garrity.

"Don't call me crazy again, Mayor," Cox said dangerously. "Or I'll be tempted to waste this shot on you. I never shot a man in the back, and I'm not starting now. But, by God, I'm going to have a chance at Horn or know why."

The telegraph key began to click, and Leggett scuttled on rheumatic legs through the shambles of the railing. In his hands, Shelly felt the cold hardness of Cullen's gun. George Cox was mad, mad as a hydrophobia skunk, and in a way it was right to kill a mad thing before it destroyed you. The odds were in his favor.

He made his eyes stay on Cox, with the girl crushed to him. Cullen still lay on the floor where Marcy had been forced to leave him when Cox made his play. The telegraph stopped, and there was only the sound of the clock, with Shelly's heartbeat racing it. He tried to think carefully, but it was hard. Twice he began to work it through, and both times he lost the thread of thought under the gaze of Cox's smoldering black eyes.

It was because of Marcy, mainly, that Cox wanted to kill him. That much was clear. Beyond that, Cox would want her to see Shelly dead or dying. So he wouldn't be likely to harm the girl with Shelly still alive. The part about not shooting a man in the back was the tough thing to figure. If Cox was far enough gone, observing any code of alleged chivalry would seem to make little difference. Yet, there would be little satisfaction for Cox doing it that way.

Assuming he was still rational, Cox would be a fool to kill Shelly in cold blood. He had the one bullet, and Larrabee or the others outside would surely get Cox. If they didn't kill him outright, he would hang. These were the things Shelly weighed in the seconds that Cox's eyes drilled into him. And at last he made up his mind.

Stooping, Shelly set the loaded gun on the

floor. Then he straightened, looked full at Marcy for an instant without seeing the man who held her, and walked slowly for the doorway and the darkness outside. Hayes Larrabee let out his breath in a wheezing gasp.

As he passed over the threshold, Shelly was sucking in his breath and feeling his guts double up. His back was to the man who had sworn revenge and in his mind he pictured Cox's arm leveling, the barrel of the gun aimed between Shelly's shoulder blades or at the back of his head.

Marcy said, "George — please — " Then Shelly was walking across the road to where his wagon stood, and no shot had torn into him. Twice in a night he had gambled with his life, and each time he had won. There would be another time, he was sure of that, but now his brain was too worn to pursue the thought further. Pushing past the men who yelled excited questions at him, he entered the jail. It was a funny thing. He had never been in a jail before in his life, and now he was in and out like a regular visitor.

"Frank Cullen," he told the doctor. "Cox beat him up in the depot. Will you come over — "

"Damn!" The doctor got to his feet and stared down at the cot where Hertzog lay. "This town has gone stark, staring mad! Clay, don't let anybody touch this man, you hear?"

As they crossed the street, Shelly watched two men moving toward the stable, and with an odd tightness in his belly realized that one of them was George Cox. At least he would ride out of town unarmed; Larrabee would see to that. But he would be back.

The doctor swore profusely when he saw Cullen, unmindful of Marcy weeping over her father and trying to make his face recognizable. And Shelly knew before the doctor said it just what he was thinking.

"You stood here and watched? And him with a bullet in that shoulder. I'll be damned. Verily, I will." Then he opened his bag and got out scissors to cut away Cullen's shirt.

Shelly turned away in shame and went outside, hearing the unguarded derision, the loud sneers, *Yellow,* someone called. *Five shots Cox gave him, and right hand against left! And Horn turned his back! Yellow!* These were no scoffing cowboys, no cattlemen roughing up a farmer. These were his own people.

He was climbing into the wagon when he heard Marcy's voice, and he almost didn't stop. Facing her would finish him, he was sure, but what did it matter as long as she was still alive? It was that way when you loved someone.

180

"Shelly?" Before he could stop her she had put her arms about him and pressed her face against his chest. Unsure of himself, he held her to him, tipping his head down until his lips touched her hair.

"Shelly — when I thought he was going to kill you . . ."

She was crying then, but it was all right because her lips lifted to his, and the wetness of her cheeks and the shudders of her sobbing were his proof. She understood. He held her and tried vainly to keep his legs from shaking.

CHAPTER 12

Cullen fought back to consciousness, trying to roll away from the clamping pain in his shoulder. He opened his eyes and saw Marcy kneeling over him, her lip caught between her teeth as she watched the doctor working at the wound.

"Daddy — Daddy. You're all right." It was half question, half-crooning insistence, as though his daughter were mothering him.

"If you two can hold him still, he'll be all right," the doctor said testily. "You can let up now, Larrabee."

Hayes Larrabee grunted and heaved himself up from Cullen. Sweat beaded his beefy face, and his eyes mirrored his abhorrence of butchered human flesh.

By twisting his neck until it hurt, Cullen could see that his shoulder was tied up crudely, the bandage already red with his blood. Oddly, there was no feeling where the bullet had been dug out; the pain centered in his right side instead.

The fight came back fuzzily now. He had watched Cox work over belligerent ranch hands and an occasional small-time rustler, with some idea of the beating the man could dole out. Now there was tardy pity for Cox's victims. He remembered the last bruising blow to his body, and the smash of what felt like a cross-tie on the back of his neck.

"You wipe his face for him, Marcy," the doctor said, wincing as he straightened and rubbed his legs. "And tell him to leave the brawling to the youngsters."

"Where's Cox?" Cullen asked thickly before his daughter could reach for the basin on the floor beside her. "He's not — "

"Don't worry," the sheriff said, mopping at his face. "He's cleared out of Trinidad by now." He had misunderstood Cullen's question.

"I owe him money," Cullen said, half to himself.

"Money, hell," the sheriff said shortly. "I reckon I should of held him till you could swear out a warrant, Cullen. The damn fool is crazy for sure."

"He had good reason," Cullen said. "I've got no call to have him jailed."

"No more call than a man has to kill an animal gone loco," the doctor snorted. "I hear he came close to shooting young Horn a minute ago, and held Marcy here as a shield while he tried."

"That's right," Larrabee said, as though in apology. "My hands were tied, Cullen. He hid behind your girl and tried to provoke Shelly into a gunfight. Made out there was a single shell in one of your guns, and he'd take that to the kid's five."

"Oh God." Cullen breathed it softly. Realizing what had happened was tearing him two ways at once.

"Beats me why he didn't shoot the boy," Larrabee said. "But Shelly just turned around and walked out. Cox had the hammer back, then he changed his mind and took off."

Cullen tried to say something, but Marcy had the cloth to his face now, sponging away blood and dirt as gently as she could. So Cox was out in the dark somewhere. It would have been easy to tell Larrabee to bring the man in — the thought of him endangering Marcy was enough of a spur. And yet Cullen could see the other side of it, too.

Cox had served him well these past years, doing jobs another man wouldn't have had the backbone to do. There was the time his foreman had waded into a drunken brawl in Gilliam's to drag Wesp out before two mule skinners could use their knives on the little man. And Cox had stuck to his guns about the farmers all the way, even when Cullen backed down and made the move he'd sworn he'd never make. There was a touch of shame tinging what he felt now as he tried to clear his head enough to get off the floor.

It throbbed as he got to his feet, the doctor on one side and Larrabee on the other, supporting him until he was oriented. He nodded, shrugging free of them.

"You still want me to send this message?" Leggett, looking cowed and yet pleased at the excitement in his depot, waved the paper.

"Of course," Cullen said. "I didn't tell you not to, did I?"

"What message?" Larrabee said quickly. "You up to something, Cullen?"

"Call it what you like," Cullen answered. "I'm telling Deems to throw in with the supporters of the relief bill."

"I'll be double-damned," the doctor said, shaking his head and snorting. "Cox's actions begin to make sense in that light. You're older than I thought."

"Daddy, I — "

"Let's leave it for now, Marcy," Cullen said, his tone flat.

"Marcy, you try to get him to rest up a couple of days, will you?" the doctor asked her. "If that shoulder looks like it's infected put on a poultice and send for me no matter what he says. Understand?"

"Yes," Marcy said. "I'll get a buggy from the stable and — "

"I can take you," Shelly Horn said. He was standing in the door, shoulders sagging and a whipped expression on his face. "I'm going out to our place now."

"Like hell!" Larrabee said. "You heard what Cox said about getting you. For the next couple of days you better stay with your folks in town. By then we'll know which way that lunatic's gonna jump."

Color drove the whiteness from the boy's face, and he took his eyes from Marcy to face Larrabee.

"I heard what they said, but I'm no coward," he protested. "I'm not afraid of Cox."

"I knew a man wasn't scared of a train once," Larrabee said with a short laugh. "Killed him just the same as if he was. You get on over and join your folks like I said. Unless you want to spend a night in jail, and that might break your ma up."

"Please, Shelly," Marcy said, and there was color in her cheeks as Cullen turned to study his daughter. "I know you're not afraid."

"All right. Mr. Cullen, thanks for sending that telegram to Austin. And if there's anything I can do — "

"You've done enough for one day, son,"

Cullen said. "Be careful, is all."

"Good night," Shelly said. He didn't say Marcy's name, but it was plain he was speaking to her and the color still burned in his cheeks as he turned and walked out into the night. The doctor nodded toward Cullen and followed Shelly out.

"Set down, Cullen," Larrabee said. "Let Marcy drive you now. Don't you try to drive with that shoulder."

"Thanks. Look, Hayes, about George Cox — "

"I figure I can take care of that if it comes up. You got some misplaced ideas about Cox, but don't worry. If he keeps his nose clean I won't bother him none. Good night, and I hope we don't have too many deaths to straighten up at the hearing!"

They sat on the worn bench facing Leggett, and Marcy held tight to her father's good arm. She seemed to be keeping the tears back with an effort, and Cullen felt the love for his daughter like an ache inside him.

"I'm proud of you, Daddy," she said. "Terribly proud."

"The wire, you mean?" he asked her. His voice was tight when he went on. "You think maybe your mother might reconsider about coming home now that I've gone over to the other camp?"

"Don't say that, Daddy," she told him, her fingers squeezing his arm. "She'd have come anyway — knowing you're hurt and needing her."

There was silence then until they heard a rig come down the street and stop outside. The clock on the wall showed nearly ten when they left the depot. It was cooler, and Cullen filled his lungs after the stale closeness of the station. He let the hostler help him into the buggy beside Marcy, and settled back as she swung the horses to head for the parsonage. He was more tired than he wanted to admit, although he was aware that some of his fatigue was apprehension about seeing Emily again.

He shouldn't have worried. Marcy went in for her, and Emily flew out to the buggy as soon as she heard Cullen was there.

"Oh, dear God, Frank! Tell me you're all right!" she pleaded.

"I'm fine, Emily," he said. "Will you come home with us? There's a lot I've got to tell you."

She kissed him lightly, ran back into the house, and returned in a few moments ready for the trip. When she got into the buggy beside him she was careful and solicitous about his shoulder. The emptiness he had carried since they parted began to ease with

188

her touch and presence. As they passed the jail, Larrabee's shout made Marcy rein up. Cullen cursed under his breath, fearful of more trouble as the sheriff walked toward them and rested a hand on the dash.

"I'm having a couple deputies ride with you, Cullen," he said. "Just in case Cox is out there in the hills someplace laying for you."

"You don't have to do that," Cullen said. "There won't be any more trouble. George is finally on his way to Montana."

"All right, don't get huffy about it. But if you aren't worried for your own skin, show some concern for your women. You can ride with an escort or wait till morning. Take your pick."

"Let's go, Marcy," Cullen said. "If your mind's made up, Sheriff, send your men along. They're going to be bored by the time they get to the ranch and back."

"That's none of your worry, Cullen. In case Cox comes around your place, you be mighty careful. Good night, ladies." Larrabee touched his hat and backed away from the buggy as two riders pulled up alongside.

"Good night, Sheriff," Emily said. "And thank you. We'll be careful."

Marcy slapped the reins, and the team moved down the street. The escort fell in behind them; Paul Clay and a rider Cullen didn't recognize. It seemed a shame to waste men's time this way. They were well out from Trinidad, nearly to the Horn place, when Marcy told her mother about the wire to Brady.

"Isn't it wonderful, Mother?" she said, and Cullen took in a deep breath. He didn't think he could stand it if they made a big thing of it. But Emily seemed to read his mind with the gift that had always mystified him.

"Yes, dear," she said, and left it at that. Cullen let out his breath.

"Don't overrate me," he said to Marcy. "I'm not so big a man that my support alone will push the measure through. Maybe it was just a foolish gesture, but after what Young Horn did — "

"You could have been killed, Frank," Emily said. She leaned her head against his good shoulder and took his hand in both of hers. "I know it's wrong to think evil, but I almost wish Hertzog would die!"

There was a bitterness in her voice that surprised Cullen, and he said almost placatingly, "It won't make much difference, Emily. He'll hang anyway. If I hadn't shot him he'd have finished me off, and maybe Shelly Horn too."

"Forgive me for all I've said, Frank," Emily said. "I was wrong in blaming you for everything. You were just doing what you had to do."

"I'm no saint," he said. "Maybe I'm what George called me. An old fool."

"Poor George," Emily said quietly. "I don't think he can help it. He just can't help it at all."

"Do you think he's really leaving, Daddy?"

"Yes. I'm sure of it." Cullen paused a moment, then went on. "I want you to hear it all, Emily. Every bit of this rotten mess."

He quickly told her everything up to the point where Cox had clubbed him down, and then Marcy finished the story. Emily caught her breath tensely when Marcy described Cox using her to shield himself from Larrabee, but she said nothing until the girl was through.

"Thank the good Lord," she breathed finally. Cullen almost said *Amen*. The fact that he even thought it surprised him.

"They all thought Shelly was a coward," Marcy said in the silence after Emily's remark. "But he did what I prayed he would do. George could have killed him no matter what the odds, but he wouldn't shoot him in the back. Somehow I knew — "

Cullen could understand, and understanding tormented him. Cox would be riding with that rage burning inside him now. He wondered if he still had the ring, and what he would do with it. Pride is a big thing, and when it's gone hate can fill the void. Cullen knew that well.

He had made a move in a direction opposite what he had sworn to follow, and he didn't think he regretted that move. But there was confusion in his mind now. A man could seldom conceive of himself as evil, just as a man hated to accept himself as a coward. Cullen wavered in a neutral region, trying to decide if he was weak or stupidly noble, and ended by rejecting both possibilities. Of only one thing he was sure — he was tired. And he was glad they were a family again. For that alone the sacrifice could be worthwhile.

The north star rode high above the mountains, but as they began the climb beyond the Horn place, Cullen was surprised to realize it had winked out. As if she were still privy to his thoughts, Emily stirred beside him.

"Is it really clouding up, Frank? There to the north?"

"Dust, more likely," he said. "I've noticed a breeze for a while. It hasn't rained for so long, Emily, I can't imagine it's about to now."

They drove on in silence, slower as they

went up the long rise. At the crest they could make out the faint wink of yellow that was the lights of the ranch. The sight was a relief to Cullen, though he wasn't sure exactly what he had feared. He favored his shoulder the best he could on the rough parts of the road, and when Marcy apologized for her driving he told her he could have done no better.

As they reached the corral, the deputy sheriff reined alongside. His voice was matter-of-fact when he told Cullen they would turn back.

"Hayes said to see you safe on your place, Cullen. I reckon this is far enough."

"Won't you come in and have some coffee?" Emily said, leaning out to look up at the deputy. "We do appreciate your riding along."

"No'm. Thanks just the same." Clay tugged at the brim of his hat and wheeled his mount. "Good night."

"I told Larrabee it was a fool's errand," Cullen said, the ache in his body edging his temper. "Drive to the house, Marcy, and you and your mother can get out. I'll take the rig to the barn."

"I can do that," Marcy said. Earl Wesp saved them the bother by limping across the yard and asking who was there.

Emily lit the lamps in the house and they

insisted that Cullen lie down on the couch while Marcy made coffee. It was near stifling at first, since the house had been shut all day. But the breeze continued, tinkling the glass chimes hanging on the porch. When Marcy brought the coffee the two of them sat by him, waiting for it to cool. There was little talk, but there seemed no need to say much. Once Cullen started to apologize for the way things had gone, but Emily cut him off with her fingers at his lips.

"It's good to be home," Marcy said at length. "More coffee, Daddy?"

"Not now," he told her, the smile numbing his hurt face.

"I'll leave the pot," she said, getting up with her cup and saucer and taking them to the kitchen. When she came back she bent over him and touched her lips softly to his, as though not to hurt him. "Good night, Daddy. I love you so much."

"Good night, Marcy. I love you, too."

Emily washed the dishes and blew out the lamp in the kitchen. He was up when she came back, standing at the screen door and looking out to where the cottonwoods rustled faintly.

"I can sleep tonight, Frank," she said as they went down the hall to their bedroom. "I've missed you so."

She helped him undress and turned back the covers. At the windows the soft curtains moved back and forth, and Emily propped them with a chair to let in more breeze. Cullen sank into the softness of the down mattress with a sigh. It *was* good to be home. Emily blew out the lamp, and he heard her move across the room in the sudden dark.

"Emily," he said when she lay beside him, "I've been a stubborn fool — "

"Shh," she said covering his mouth with hers. She was soft against him, and the wall that had been was gone. No shame, no more feeling of guilt or error. Only the deep, abiding love of two people content with and sure of each other. Later, she slept like a child, and the breeze from the window dried the tears on his face. Tears that weren't all Emily's.

The sound of the rain woke him, but it was almost like a dream as he swung his feet to the floor and eased carefully from the bed. Large drops, with the gathering wind behind them, pelted his legs and then the rest of him as he moved to close the window. This was no dream, no dust storm. He whispered Emily's name, but there was no answer and he left her sleeping.

He stood outside in the wetness and tilted

his head back. Rain bathed his face and ran in rivulets down his body. To the north, lightning flashed, and a moment later he heard and felt the deep, distant mutter of thunder. This God of Emily's was a strange one. He wondered if Jethro Horn would feel the rain down under the sod, and a bitter sadness for the farmer swept him.

CHAPTER 13

Shelly Horn woke to the delighted shouting of youngsters slopping in the mud and rain outside the window. Rubbing his eyes, he blinked in the dark room, unable to believe it was real. But when he unlatched the board window and swung it open, gusty wind drove the rain cold and hard against his face, taking his breath away. Behind him, the door creaked open and he heard Fred Palmer's voice.

"Goin' to sleep your life away, boy? It's past eight already, dark as it is!"

"Rain," Shelly said. *"Rain!"* He shut the window and turned to face the farmer who was putting them up.

"It's rain, I reckon. Just like your pa said it would come when it finally did. The river's actin' like one, for a change. Near bank full and risin' fast. How'd you sleep through it, Shelly?"

"I've dreamed about rain before," Shelly said. He could see well enough to find his clothes, and he began to dress. Actually he remembered nothing since falling into bed last night, and the fact of rain was a welcome jolt. Almost as if God knew Shelly had reached the end of his rope and sent it so he could begin again.

"I'll go tell Miz Palmer to fry some meat and warm the biscuits," Palmer said, his voice filled with excitement. "You want to wash up, Shelly, just hang your head out the window!"

The place the Palmers had found was a board shack no bigger than the Horn soddy. Shelly had to push his way into the kitchen, but the squeezing together didn't seem to bother the women. His sister Trissa washed a plate for Shelly and slid it onto the table as Mrs. Palmer opened the oven door with the corner of her apron.

"It's raining, Shelly," his mother said, staring out the open door to where Billie Jo played with the Palmer kids. "Your pa always promised me it would. Now maybe there'll be flowers can grow out to his grave."

"That's right, Ma." Shelly sat down on the bench and inhaled the smell of meat and buttered biscuits. The coffee Mrs. Palmer poured into his cracked cup boiled and sizzled over the lip of the pot. Palmer leaned in the doorway, warming his hands around his coffee cup, a smile akin to worship wrinkling his red face.

"We'll get on back to our place, I reckon,"

Shelly said between bites. "This rain's going to last a while, and the young ones can't stay outside all the time. We've crowded you all long enough for one visit."

"Nothing of the kind," Mrs. Palmer protested dutifully. "We're still beholden to you folks and — "

"If I'm going to catch the train, Shelly," his mother started, but Shelly shook his head.

"It can wait a day or so. Maybe there won't be a train if it keeps coming down like this."

Thunder smashed against the house then, and one of the Palmer girls squealed in fright and fled to the bedroom. Billie Jo raced into the kitchen, splashing water like a wet puppy, with the Palmer boys right back of her.

"Billie Jo!" her mother cried. "Don't track all that mud in Mrs. Palmer's clean house! Now you just wipe your feet off, and then get your things together. Shelly says we got to go out to our place today."

"You can suit yourself, boy," Palmer said, moving to the stove to drop his cup into the dishpan. "We can make out all right — though there won't likely be any trains for a while. I was down to the barbershop listening to the talk, and Leggett says there's a bridge out east. Wouldn't surprise me none if the river floods before night if this keeps up."

"Then Joe Crisp and the others in the bottoms better start bailing," Shelly said, getting up from the table. "That was mighty good, Miz Palmer, and I surely appreciate what you've done for us. Maybe someday we can pay it back."

"This rain keeps comin' down, and we'll likely be crowdin' in on *you!*" Palmer said, laughing. "Lucky you're on higher ground, Shelly."

"Could I trouble you for the loan of some canvas to keep the rain off the womenfolk?" Shelly asked as he waited for his mother and sisters to get ready.

"You just take our wagon, boy. We ain't apt to go no place in this weather!"

"I'd be much obliged. Ready, Ma? Mr. Palmer's letting us take their wagon so you and the girls won't get wet."

He drove from inside the wagon, getting wet even then. The road was a gully of churned mud, and water stood in the fields, which were ruffled by wind from the dark clouds. There was lightning farther back in the hills, and Shelly knew that water from the higher ground was coursing down to help swell the river. Trinidad looked deserted, with no sign of life save the feeble glow of lamps back of boarded windows.

Half a dozen horses cowered at the tie

rail in front of Gilliam's bar, tails to the wind and hides sleek with wet. Shelly had to keep prodding with the whip to prevent the borrowed team from quitting cold. Crossing the river, he heard the women gasp at sight of the roily dark water barely a foot below the planks. Parallel to them the railroad trestle gleamed dully, and two laborers wrestled awkwardly with sledges, paying no mind to the wagon as it crossed the river.

They reached the soddy with no trouble, and here, even on higher ground, the fields were soaked deep. Shelly thought bitterly of the choking dust and the hard-baked ground that had met the burial picks in the cemetery. The rain that could save the farmers had come late; maybe too late. And now it seemed bent on drowning the land that wanted only nourishment.

"You're not going back!" his mother exclaimed as she sat in a rocker and caught her breath. "Shelly, wait until the storm lets up."

"They may need help if the river jumps the bank, Ma," he told her. "You'll be all right till I get back, won't you?"

"We'll be fine," Trissa said. "Mrs. Palmer gave us some cornbread and beans to bring along. And there's wood in the box for the fire. You be careful, Shelly. Please."

"Sure. Nothing can happen to me today except maybe drowning," he grinned, "and I'll manage to keep out of the river. I'd hate to see Crisp and that bunch washed into the next county, even if they should have known better than to build there."

"We'll be all right," Trissa repeated. "After all, we've got Billie Jo here to help out." She patted the little girl on the head and hugged her to herself.

"Goodby, Ma," Shelly said, kissing her on the cheek at the door. "I don't think you'll have any visitors in this weather, but don't let anybody in. The shotgun is loaded."

"I wish you would stay," she told him, almost in tears. "But I guess you ought to go help out. Come home as quick as you can — we'll have a nice supper."

He slapped the reins to the team, seeing the sweat steam in spite of the rain. They stepped out faster going back, with the lighter load and a downhill pull, and he made good time to town. A quarter of a mile short of the bridge, he frowned and squinted against the driving rain trying to decide what it was he saw.

Nearly to the river, he realized what had happened. The railroad trestle had collapsed! It lay nearly submerged in the rushing water, a huge timber dam that already was raising the level of the water upstream. Dozens of men were fighting and cursing in the mud as they sought to secure ropes to the structure and drag it clear.

"You there!" someone yelled. "Hey, pull that team over this way!"

Shelly made out the large bulk of Mayor Garrity and swung the team obediently. As he climbed down from the seat, eager hands unhitched the animals and led them toward the riverbank. Following, Shelly spotted Fred Palmer shoveling dirt from a wagon as he helped build up a dike against the mounting water.

"You were right, Shelly," the farmer said, grunting with the exertion. "The river's already backing up into the bottomland! Grab a shovel, eh?"

There was no keeping track of time after that. Not by the sun, for the sky stayed a sullen, wind-torn mass of black cloud that deluged the already flooding land. Even the pangs of hunger in his belly were lost in the pain of killing effort. Until Garrity was ready with a dozen heavy ropes secured to the trestle, Shelly heaved dirt shoulder to shoulder with Palmer. In midafternoon every available back strained with the teams as they slipped and stumbled in the mud.

Garrity, or someone, had planned well. The ropes angled downstream of the trestle, so that the pull of the lines was in the same direction as the force of the river against the timbers.

"Heave, damn you!" the mayor bawled. "Heave if you don't want the whole town to float to Kingdom Come!"

"Heave?" Palmer repeated thickly as he pulled on the rope. "I know I'm ruptured already!"

Then the ropes eased with a suddenness that made Shelly fear they had parted. But a shout of triumph went up over the sound of rain and rushing water as the trestle yielded. Once started, it moved ever faster, until finally it pointed downstream with fragments of timbers jutting out of the dark water. They moored it like a recalcitrant whale to the trees bordering the river, and then most of the men fell where they stood.

Shelly was dimly aware of gulping hot coffee and trying to swallow cold biscuit and meat. When his head cleared and breathing was easy again, he was surprised to find the rain had all but stopped.

"Thank God for that," Palmer said. "Yesterday I never thought I'd be glad to see it *quit* raining. Right now I'd as soon burn up as drown!"

They walked through the mud to Palmer's place, and there was a hot pride in Shelly in spite of the agony of the hours of killing work. For weeks the men of Trinidad had been listless and at loose ends, listening at street corners to any rabble-rouser who came along. Half of them ready to give up in this land God had already forsaken. And now they had been united by even more hardship! They had lasted out the drought, and they had licked the flood. All that was lacking to make it a triumph was Jethro Horn himself.

"You'll stay the night, Shelly," Palmer said. "Man would be a fool to go slopping out there tonight, tired as you must be."

"Put me down for a fool," Shelly said. "I couldn't get any more tired than I am already. Thanks for the offer, but I'll ride out to the place and make sure Ma and the girls are all right."

"You got more backbone than brains, boy. But it's your back." Palmer shrugged.

It was past eight o'clock when he left Palmer standing in his doorway. The rain had stopped completely now, though it would be a long time before the ground would reflect that, and he even thought he saw stars twinkling to the north. His belly was full, the supper Mrs. Palmer insisted he eat a pleasant warmth inside him. He rode wearily, yet with content. It was a satisfying weariness, and he could ease up now. Or so he thought until he passed Gilliam's bar.

"That you, Shelly Horn?" He recognized the bartender's voice and made out the man's bulk in the doorway.

"That's right," Shelly said, reining up. "You want me?"

"Unless Larrabee already told you, kid. Cox was in here this afternoon looking for you. He was drunk, and I didn't tell him anything. But you better be on the watch."

"Thanks. I will." The tightness was back, and he cursed himself for being so smug a moment ago. He couldn't let up for a minute.

"I'd ask you in for a beer, Shelly," Gilliam said hesitantly, "but under the circumstances, maybe — "

Shelly had never been in Gilliam's or any bar. A week ago he would have answered such an offer coldly, but something in the man's tone got through to him. It was a friendly gesture, and there was respect in it too.

"Maybe another time, Mr. Gilliam," he said. "And thanks for the tip."

"You got a gun?"

"No. It's all right. I'll be careful."

"The hell. Hold up a minute." Gilliam turned inside and was back a moment later. He handed a gun up to Shelly, a pearl-handled Colt that was smooth and heavy.

"The Bible is a good book, Shelly," the bartender said. "But you shove this in your belt, too. You've had enough grief for a while."

"Thanks. Thanks a lot." Shelly slid the gun into the pocket of the coat Palmer had lent him and touched his heels to the horse. The warmth in his belly was gone now.

When he crossed the river he could hear the rushing gurgle of water beneath him, but the level had dropped far below its crest. Joe Crisp would be out some topsoil, but he still had a farm and a roof over his head. Part of Shelly's mind tried to pursue the thought of what rain could mean to the country. They could hang on now that there was some water. The farm Jethro Horn had killed himself for might even do well, if this storm was an omen.

But the sudden worry about Cox drove any plans from him. Several times he felt for the gun, once even taking it out to check if it was loaded. Gilliam had done a strange thing for a man who depended largely on cowboys for his trade. It was more confused than that, with Cox drunk on Gilliam's whiskey more than likely.

Shelly rode at a fast trot, stopping now and then to listen and study the ground ahead. In the open country an ambush would hardly be likely, but he was taking no chances. When he came in sight of the lighted kitchen window of the soddy, he reined up and dismounted. For perhaps five minutes he stood there, straining to hear or see something out of the ordinary. Finally he snorted in disgust at his caution and climbed back in the saddle. He was being an old woman.

He booted the horse into a gallop and held it for the rest of the way. Half the sky was clear now and the silver of moon made a faint light. He slid out of the saddle at the door and suddenly heard the sound of sobbing. With a choked cry, he pounded up the steps and slammed against the door.

"Ma! Ma, it's me, Shelly. Open the door, Ma!"

The sobbing stopped and he recognized Billie Jo's small voice. She fumbled at the bolt on the door, and then it swung in with Shelly's weight; the child flung herself on him, crying as if her heart would break.

"Shelly — oh, Shelly, I thought you'd never come!"

Fear made him angry, and he shook her roughly. She lost her breath then, and he had to wait until she could speak again.

"Billie Jo, for God's sake quit it! You hear? Where's Ma and Trissa, Billie Jo? Speak up now, or I'll paddle you."

"Shelly — Ma — " She caught her breath in apparent terror and he shook her.

"Billie Jo! It's all right. I'm here now. Where's Ma?"

"It's Trissa, Shelly. She went to the barn to see if the hens was laying. I heard her scream, Shelly, like she was half-kilt. Then Ma ran out. I — "

"Ma!" Shelly shouted. "Ma, where are you?"

"The man came in then," Billie Jo got out at last, her eyes large and vacant. "I hid in the bed. He left the note, and after a while Ma came in with her head cut open. She took a pan of water back out to the barn and told me to bolt the door. Oh, Shelly!" She caught him around the legs with a shrill scream of terror, and he had to shake her to get her loose.

He was yelling like a crazy man when he reached the barn, but there was no answer. He yanked the door open to find his mother sitting on the floor next to the stall, cradling Trissa's head on her lap. There was a quilt covering the girl, and her face was bruised and cut. Shelly heard himself swear aloud as though it weren't him at all.

"Is she — dead, Ma?"

"No, Shelly. Not dead." She rocked the

girl gently, crooning under her breath. "When she had all she could stand, she fainted."

"Cox?" Shelly asked. He was shaking so hard he laid his hands along his thighs to steady them. "Was it George Cox, Ma?"

"Yes." She nodded, and looked up without seeing him at all. "He kept rambling on about Marcy Cullen, all the while he was . . . Lord, my poor Trissa."

He understood then. All in one quick flash he knew what Cox meant by this vicious attack, and his hand went to the gun in the coat pocket. His mother seemed to see him for the first time.

"The note, Shelly. Don't you pay any mind. It's a trap — "

"I'll kill him, Ma! Don't you see? I've got to kill him now."

"Or let him kill you?" Her voice rose, shrill in the dim barn. "There's two dozen fathers in town will see him hanging at the end of a rope. Shelly, don't leave us!"

He got to his feet, staring down at the colorless face of his sister, swallowing as he saw the ugly bruise above her eyes and the slanting laceration down her right cheek. Being a man, he was ashamed at what a man had done, and grateful for the quilt his mother had covered Trissa with. Drunk or sober, Cox was clever, terribly clever. It was a trap, of course, but a trap no man could evade. Deaf to his mother's pleading, Shelly left the barn and headed for the house. The note would tell him how he could find George Cox and revenge. It was a spiteful God up there in heaven, he thought with hot anger.

CHAPTER 14

Cullen ate breakfast with Emily a little bit after eight o'clock. He had been up since four, talking with the men in the bunkhouse before they went out to relieve the others, and his body ached with tiredness and the hurt from the beating Cox had given him. He had spent most of the previous day in the saddle during the downpour, and besides the physical drain that had been, he had watched helplessly while a dozen of his cattle drowned. But it had rained, and it was as though the wetness of it stirred something in him he had thought dead, like the budding of a stump in spring after a long, freezing winter.

"You'd better go back to bed, Frank," Emily told him as she poured coffee in his cup. She rested her hand lightly on his bandaged shoulder. "And I still think we should go into town and let the doctor have another look at this."

"Doctor, hell. Emily, I've got to stay on the place to try to pull this mess back into shape. There's cows scattered from hell to breakfast out there. Hasn't been a stampede like that for years."

"Just the same, you should have gone along with Marcy and had the dressing changed. If it should infect — "

"I'll spit tobacco juice on it," he said impatiently. "I told you I'd rest today. All I have to do is pay off that well-drilling crew and then help Wesp in the barn for a while. But don't expect me to sit on my behind when the boys are in the saddle around the clock."

"All right, Frank. All right. Just be as easy on yourself as you can, please. You're going to see the doctor tomorrow if I have to drag you there."

"Tomorrow's different, Emily. I don't like the idea of Marcy going off by herself anyhow. There's several birds I can kill with one stone tomorrow. Right now, though — " He broke off at the sound of a horse slopping through the still sodden yard.

"Do finish your breakfast!" Emily said in a provoked tone. "You half starved yourself yesterday, Frank."

"That's likely Nelson back from the Tanks. I'll just be a minute."

He rose heavily and went out onto the porch, eager for the report on conditions to the north. The sight of the man in the saddle drew him up short, and he leaned his weight against the post by the stairs.

Cox hadn't shaved since Cullen had seen him last. His clothes were mud-caked, and from the look of his eyes he was hung over. The six-guns bulking at his waist made Cullen feel suddenly naked, unarmed as he was. For part of a second he was about to go inside and buckle on his own belt, but that would have drawn Emily into it. He decided to play it out the way it had started.

"Hello, George." He went halfway down the steps. "Something I can do for you?"

"You can pay me off, Cullen," the man said brusquely. "You owe me a hundred dollars."

"I know that," Cullen told him. "I would have paid you in town the other night, only — "

"You got what was due you, I'd say. I'm satisfied. Except I got those wages coming."

"I'll make out a check. I did once before, but — "

"Make it paper money, Cullen. And I'll come in. I could do with a drink." Cox blinked and pinched at his eyes with a dirty hand. As he slid from the saddle, he swayed against the animal so that it shied. "Stand steady, damn you!" he said.

There was no sign from the kitchen; Emily

must have thought it was Nelson and gone about her chores. Cullen swallowed, dry-mouthed, and led the way to his office off the front room. Cox shoved the door closed with his boot, and sank into the big leather chair.

"We got our rain, eh, Cullen?" Cox's voice was flat and bitter. "Now that it's too late, we get one hell of a rain!"

"Here's *two* hundred dollars," Cullen said, sliding the drawer closed. "I'm sorry the way things came out. Do you — ?"

"Your cottonpicking friends got a bellyful of rain, you know that? Damn trestle caved in, and the river flooded the bottoms. Ain't that a goddam shame?"

"I've got plenty trouble right here on the ranch," Cullen said. He set the money down on the arm of the chair Cox was sitting in and walked across the room for the bottle in the cabinet. The last time they had a drink together was only a short while back, and Cox had sat in the same chair while they talked about the herd Cullen was going to buy.

"Everybody's got troubles, Cullen," Cox said, opening his eyes and reaching for the bottle as Cullen came toward him. "Don't cry on my shoulder."

"I'm short-handed, George. There's cows

drowned, more of them bogged and going to die. The boys have been fighting like hell since the first cloudburst, but it's a losing battle. Look, we could forget what happened — "

"By God, Cullen, you *have* gone soft in your old age! I beat the devil out of you and you turn the other cheek? I guess I didn't make it clear I didn't hire on to blow nesters' snotty noses for them. You're dumber than I thought." He tilted the bottle.

"I'm still running cattle," Cullen said desperately. Part of the dream was back now, and he grabbed at it. If Cullen could swallow his pride, maybe his ex-foreman could do the same. "There's not a man on the place to match you, George. You know I'm not making a lot this year, and maybe a man can never get rich at it, but we could discuss the money — "

"There's not that much money," Cox said. "Not now there isn't. God damn you, Cullen!" He got to his feet, his fist doubled about the neck of the bottle, and Cullen sat down. Then Cox subsided with a short laugh. He picked up the money with his left hand and spread the bills between thumb and fingers. Satisfied, he shoved them into his pocket.

"I'm sorry it didn't work out about

Marcy," Cullen said. "That disappointed me too. But she's stubborn — all women are."

"Don't apologize, Cullen. I wouldn't marry her now if she was gold plated. Save your breath if you got nothing better to talk about." He stoppered the bottle and put it under his arm, then wiped at his mouth with his sleeve. "We'll just call it even, eh?"

"All right, George," Cullen said. Something in the words, or maybe it was the nervous tension of the man, stabbed a warning into him, and he thought of Marcy alone on the road to Trinidad. "One thing, though, you get any funny ideas about Marcy and I promise you I won't turn the other cheek again. Understand?"

"Noble," Cox said, turning his head to spit in the direction of the cuspidor. "Real noble. And what do you figure to get crossing your heifer with a damn lintback farmer? I'd kind of like to hang around to see the runty litter they'll turn out, but I can't stomach any more. One little chore, and I'm heading north. Thanks for goddam little, Frank Cullen, and I'll see you in hell one of these days."

With the bottle under his arm, Cox strode heavily from the room. Cullen followed him, nerves tight now with worry for his daughter. Cox had seemed to bear down on the word "marry" a while ago, and the look in his bloodshot eyes was that of a man past caring.

"Frank?" Emily half opened the kitchen door and her voice trailed off as she recognized Cox.

"It's all right," Cullen told her, praying she would go back inside. Instead, she came across the porch to put her arm about him as he watched Cox slide the bottle into his saddlebag and then pull himself into the saddle.

"Like I said, Cullen," the swaying rider called. "I'll see you in hell one of these days!" Then he touched the spurs to the horse's flanks and rode full tilt out of the yard, spraying the flock of domineckers aside in a squawking flurry.

"Frank," Emily said, almost whispering, "why didn't you call me? Or some of the boys. He might have come to kill you!"

"It's not me I'm worried about, Emily," Cullen told her. "I knew you shouldn't have let Marcy go alone."

"Oh, dear God!" Her fingers clawed into his arm and he pulled quickly away. "Frank, what will we do?"

"You can pray," Cullen said. "Pray that I'm jumping at the wrong conclusion. Meantime I'd better go along just to make sure."

From the porch he bawled at Wesp to saddle a horse, then went inside for his gunbelt, vest, and hat. He thumbed shells into empty loops in the belt as he went toward the barn. The wound in his shoulder had come alive again, aching deeply, and fatigue was a weight driving his boot heels into the muddy ground.

He heard Wesp curse, then hoofs thudded and the little man came around the corner leading a black horse. Wesp's forehead wrinkled, and there was irritation in his voice.

"I thought you was going to wait for the well drillers." He scowled as Cullen pulled himself up.

"Quit thinking, if it bothers you that much," Cullen flung back at him. "If Nelson or any of the rest of the boys show up, tell them to trail me to Trinidad. I may be tracking trouble."

"Hell, Boss! Wait a second and I'll ride with you." Eagerness sparked the handyman's face, and Cullen was ashamed of himself.

"No. You stick here at the place and see that Mrs. Cullen does too. If Cox comes back, be sure he doesn't get out of line."

"I didn't know that was *Cox*," the limping Wesp said in surprise. "I'd of give you a hand sooner."

"Frank! Wait!"

It was Emily, coming down the steps of the porch. Impatiently Cullen wheeled the black and kneed him toward the house.

"Don't try to stop me, Emily," he yelled. "There's no other way to — "

"I'm not stopping you, Frank Cullen! You forgot this." It was the Winchester she handed up to him, and the look in her eyes was as grim and fiercely protective as Cullen felt. He smiled ruefully and leaned down with an effort to kiss her.

"Be careful," she said. "Please. I'm praying."

"Goodby, Emily. I won't be long." But he was remembering what Cox had said about meeting him in hell one day.

He followed the fresh tracks in the soft ground easily once he was well clear of the ranchhouse. Cox was riding fast, and the knowledge strung Cullen tighter because the tracks led toward town. It was hard to believe his ex-foreman would molest his daughter, likely the whole thing was just Cullen's wild imaginings brought on by all that had happened these last few days. But then he had never thought Cox would turn on him either.

Pride and the desire for revenge made a man do crazy things. And Cox had little to revenge him yet. Besides, he was at least half-drunk, with a bottle along to finish the job. If he should overtake Marcy — That could be the chore he spoke of. Or — Cullen tried hard not to think it — he might already have encountered the girl on his ride *to* the ranch. He rowelled the horse again, squinting anxiously ahead for a sign of the rider he trailed.

He spotted Cox about four miles from the ranch. At first he wasn't sure of his man, but when he was near enough to make out Cox and the horse he rode, breath whistled out of Cullen in relief. Slacking his pace, he stayed a quarter-mile behind just to be sure. Marcy must be nearly to Trinidad by now with the food she had insisted on taking, along with medicine against the possibility of an epidemic after the flood. Cullen had scoffed, but there was admiration for his daughter's concern. Cox had said the bottoms were flooded, and cholera would be all the town needed on top of drought and flood.

Up ahead, the rider pulled up and dismounted. Cullen angled for the cover of a scrubby clump of trees and watched, expecting Cox to take a drink from the bottle. Instead he relieved himself and then climbed back into the saddle. When he rode again, it was to the north, and Cullen smiled in satisfaction. Cox had said he was leaving, and it looked as if he meant it. Montana, he had said before, and it fitted. He had his money and the promise of a job up there. Breathing easier, Cullen wished him well.

He was about to turn for home when he saw another rider in the distance, apparently coming from town. Curiosity made Cullen ride toward him, eager for news of Trinidad. With no reason for caution, he was almost on top of Shelly Horn before he saw the gun in the boy's hand, its barrel leveled at him.

"Easy, son!" he called, raising both hands high. "Put up the hardware, I'm peaceable!"

"Sorry, Mr. Cullen," Shelly said. "I can't take chances now." He shoved the gun back into the top of his pants, and it was only then Cullen noticed the etched bitterness on the nester's face. What he read there was the deadly will to murder, and the next question jolted him back against the cantle. "Have you seen George Cox?" Shelly said.

"Cox?" Cullen turned involuntarily to look toward the rise where he had last seen his ex-foreman. There was only the bare horizon now, and as he swung his eyes back on Horn, the boy's gaze jerked back to him disappointedly. "He was at my place just a while ago. Why?"

"Because I'm going to kill him," Shelly said, his voice shaking on the edge of control. "Kill him!"

"Calm down, boy. Everything's all right

now. I forgave what he did. You can at least forget it."

"Forget rape?" Shelly demanded. "Did he go that way?" The boy gestured toward the trail forking off to the north.

"Rape?" The word grated thick and unclean on Cullen's lips, and he was suddenly sick to his stomach. "Oh God. Marcy."

"Not Marcy, Mr. Cullen. My sister Trissa." The voice was steadier now and toneless.

"When?" Cullen said, trying not to show the relief he felt, and thinking of Cox slouched in the chair in his office, drinking his liquor and sneering at him.

"Last night. I would have gone after him sooner, but the ground was too wet to tell anything. In the note he said to come to the old stage station up there." He pointed again. "You saw him?"

"Yes, Shelly, I saw him. He's headed there now." Cullen was staring in amazement. "This note — he left a note?"

"After he did it to her, and after he hit my mother with a shovel. Yes, that's when he wrote the note. He said if I wanted to do anything about it to show up at the ruins at ten this morning. Alone, or he'd ride on and I'd never catch him."

"You fool! It's a trick to kill you! He wouldn't shoot you in the back, and he couldn't rile you enough that time in the depot. Shelly, you haven't got a chance in a hundred against his gun now."

"I've backed and dodged long enough," the boy said. "Now I have to do this. I'm going to kill him, and if I die, too, it won't matter."

"What about Marcy?" Cullen asked abruptly. "She left to go into town this morning — "

"She came by the place. I guess she's still there. When she saw Trissa she started to cry and said she wished it was her. She didn't stop me, Mr. Cullen, so don't you try! This is my fight. I'm not as handy with guns as you, but I'm not as charitable either, so maybe that balances it out."

"Shelly, don't walk into this trap. I'm trying to help you, son."

"If you really want to help, ride into town and get the sheriff and the undertaker. They're both going to get work this day."

The boy was past reason, Cullen knew. The glazed, tortured look in Shelly's eyes reflected all he had taken, and Cox's last vicious act had pushed him the rest of the way. For young Horn there was now only one road: the road into a trap as rotten as it was clever. If the boy had used his head, a posse might have been riding now for

Cox. But the man was either smart enough to count on Shelly's reaction or too drunk to realize the risk. Either way, it was the same.

"What good will it do your sister if you get yourself killed?" he asked.

"You could as well say what good will it do her if I manage to kill him," Shelly said icily. "I can't argue it with you — I don't aim to. I'm beholden to you, I reckon, and maybe I better just say goodby."

Shelly eased his mount closer and stuck his hand out toward Cullen. Anger raged up in Cullen against his helplessness, and then as his hand closed over the firm calloused one of the nester, he knew what he had to do.

With all the strength in him, he jerked hard. He read the stunned look on Shelly's face, and then triumphantly completed the job of hauling him clear of the saddle. As the boy fell with a cry between the horses, Cullen reined clear and then swung around the far side of the scrawny animal the nester rode. With the straw hat he had grabbed from the boy as he fell, he swatted the animal and got him moving as Shelly scrambled up from the mud.

"Damn you, Cullen, come back here!" The crack of the gun came down the wind to Cullen, and he held his breath as he grabbed for the reins of the riderless horse. He hadn't thought the boy would go as far as shooting at him. But it was a chance he had to take, and in seconds he was out of range. When he looked back, the boy was slogging gamely after him in the mud.

CHAPTER 15

As Cullen rode north along the trail toward the abandoned stage station there was time to think about what he would do when he came up against George Cox. The significance of what his one-time foreman had done was registering in his mind with revulsion. He had never considered Cox as lily white, of course. Several times at trail's end he had watched the man select a girl from some honky-tonk to bed down with for a night. It was a thing he didn't remind himself of, a thing he would never tell Emily. But what he had done to the Horn girl . . .

Rape was a filthy business and Cullen could well understand Shelly's blind urge to vengeance. In the seconds he had feared that his own daughter had been ravished, the cry of "Kill" rushed hot and angry from deep inside him. Small wonder that Cox had insisted he couldn't stay on. The town would band almost as a man to track him down now, and it would end with a rope at best.

Shelly Horn had been about to shoot it out with Cox, and in the first rush of anger

Cullen felt the same way. He had put the straw hat of Shelly Horn on his own head as a disguise, thinking to kill Cox himself in a gunfight. But time and the wind from the west had a cooling effect on him, and he wet his lips and slowed the pace of the black he rode.

He could just make out the rough outline of the sod building that once housed a hostler and his wife, and sheltered stage passengers while they ate or spent a night along the way. The sight of it and the knowledge that Cox was waiting there to draw one last bit of satisfaction chilled Cullen's belly. He was getting old, and age and his hurts plagued him. Or was it mostly fear?

If he simply warned Cox off, using the Winchester if he had need of it, he could go back and tell Shelly Horn that Cox had fled from the duel he set up. There would be the young nester's wrath, but that was a small thing compared to a life, or maybe two lives — Horn's and Cullen's both.

A man's mind can twist and dodge and turn to evade the truth, and Cullen wondered where it really lay in this case. Was he showing a yellow streak or just being sensible? He wasn't the law, if he managed to best Cox in a gunfight by some miracle, would it be any the less murder than if he simply drew down on him with the rifle from beyond handgun range?

He cursed angrily as the distance between him and the crumbling building lessened in spite of his slowed pace. Squinting, he tried to find his quarry, but there was no sign of the man or even of his mount. Cox must have watched his back-trail, remembering his challenge to Horn with a cunning his sodden face had belied.

To the north and west there was a dark line of cloud, and the wind from that direction was moist. There was going to be more rain, and the realization would have excited Cullen except for the task ahead of him. He began a bitter snort, lifting his eyes higher to where the sky was still pale blue. He had been about to complain to the God Emily clung to, but instead he found his lips moving in prayer. A prayer for an answer to the showdown he was riding to.

"That's far enough, Cullen! Pull up, damn you!"

Cox's voice broke across Cullen's consciousness with rude force, and he sawed back on the reins in a startled reflex action, sweeping right and left with his eyes in an effort to spot the ambush.

"You must figure me for a fool or else blind drunk," the voice went on, and then

Cox stepped into view from behind brush, off the trail to the left. "That getup wouldn't fool a half-smart steer. Get your hands up over your head!"

Cullen complied, watching Cox come toward him with a gun in each of his hands. The man was dead sober, and somehow he had shaken the fatigue Cullen had noticed back at the ranch. He stopped a dozen paces off, close enough now that the wrinkles bunching his eyebrows showed.

"Now, easy with the left hand," he commanded, gesturing with the gun in his own right. "Loosen your belt and just let it and the guns drop in the mud unless you want me to open up a hole in your guts."

With his gaze riveted on Cox, Cullen obeyed. He fumbled over the buckle, but then the belt slipped free and the guns thudded into the soft ground. The black started jumpily, but Cullen caught him short with his knees, feeling as he did the stock of the Winchester. Cox didn't seem to notice.

"I've been watching you with glasses, Cullen. What'd you do with young Horn, and why the straw lid? You wouldn't be aiming to fight his battles for him, would you?"

"You would have nailed Shelly right here, wouldn't you?" Cullen asked. "Not even given him the chance in a hundred he figured he'd have."

"Don't do no preaching. It's late for that, and you ain't no preacher anyhow, Cullen. In fact, you're not a goddam bit better than you just accused me of being. You figured to bluff it out as the kid and drill me!"

"I was going to give you a break you maybe don't have coming, George," Cullen said slowly, thinking twice as fast as he talked. "I bluffed the boy so I could beat a posse here and warn you to get on a horse and put the miles back of you. The town didn't take kindly to what Shelly says you did last night."

"I said, don't preach!" Cox shouted. "And you're a liar from the word go. You came up here to pass as that damned lintback and take me off guard long enough to get me. You strung me long enough; don't take me for a fool now."

"Why did you do it?" Cullen asked, tentatively lowering his right arm. Cox made no protest and Cullen rubbed at the pain in his left shoulder. "Or was Horn lying about his sister?"

"What do you think?" Cox asked, laughing shortly. "A man gets lonesome waiting for the boss's daughter, Cullen. Tell you what, I'd have showed Marcy what she missed out on if I could have found her last night. Only she wouldn't likely hold a candle to that filly I tied into instead. Besides, I figured the farm boy was bound to come running when his sister got roughed up. Marcy, now, he might of figured she invited the attention. You know."

"I had you wrong, Cox. I'm cursing myself for that now." Cullen's breathing came hard, whistling in and out of his nostrils as he glared at Cox.

"It didn't have to be this way, you know. It could of been a whole hell of a lot different, Cullen. That song and dance you fed me — I believed it all. I was a fool for a long time, and you know, I still think it could of worked?" An odd, wistful quality was suddenly in Cox's face and his voice as he closed half the distance between them and slid the gun in his left hand into its holster.

"Yes, sir, I could've run your place for you the way it ought to be run. And you with grandchildren to be proud of. Kids with rancher blood in them. Only . . ." He trailed off, and his face went bleak and hard again.

"What are you going to do now?" Cullen asked. There was disgust in him now, but no fear. Just helpless anger at the trap he'd let himself into.

"As well a sheep as a lamb, they say," Cox quoted. He thumbed back the hammer on the gun in his hand and the black hole in its barrel lifted to point at Cullen. "So I guess I'll shoot you in the belly and go back and do the same for Horn. I figure you cut across his trail and somehow foxed him into this business. So he won't be far down the slope. After that, I'll have nothing to keep me here, Cullen. Nothing at all."

"Don't be a fool," Cullen got out as he watched Cox with desperate intentness. "You've disarmed me — you've got a start. I was lying about the posse. Ride out while you can."

"I said no preaching," Cox snapped. "You want to pray, get busy with it. I don't see any way out of you having to die."

"Cox, so far you haven't done murder. Why not — "

"All right. If you don't have any praying in you, climb down out of there. On the other side, away from the guns in the muck. I won't take any chances now."

"Cox — " Cullen started desperately.

"Down!" Cox motioned with the gun.

Cullen clamped his jaws. He had seldom thought of death, but now that it was close it took strength not to beg. He let his shoulders sag and leaned his weight to the right stirrup. With Cox watching him close, he lifted his leg clear and stepped down, the horse between them.

"Make a break for it, if you want, Cullen. That way you'll get it in the back of the head. Might be better than — "

Cullen had the stock of the Winchester in his right hand now, and he slapped hard on the black's rump with the other. The sound of the animal's lunge merged with Cox's taunt, and then Cullen faced him across the muddy trail with the Winchester leaping upward. The blast of it jolted against his ears and his shoulder, but there was no pain as he could almost feel the slug tear into the flesh of the man who had been his right hand for so long.

The handgun fired wild as Cox clutched his middle and staggered forward. His face showed only surprise as yet, and he reached automatically for his other gun while his right thumb worked at the hammer of the gun he had fired once. Some vestige of pity froze Cullen's finger on the trigger until a second closer shot from the gun in Cox's hand made it tighten convulsively. The second slug from the rifle made a small black hole above Cox's nose and he fell at Cullen's feet.

He had watched men die before, but this time was different. A wave of nausea buckled his legs under him, and he went to his knees, supporting himself by holding onto the barrel of the Winchester that dug stock down into the mud. There was searing pain in his arms, but he held on and watched the last of life manifest itself in the writhing of the man who could as well have killed him seconds ago.

With his left hand he tried weakly to lift Cox's face from the mud and roll him to his back, but he gave it up when the scene before him began to tilt and blur. Cullen pulled upright and shook his head to clear away the dizziness. When he could walk, he stumbled half-blindly down the trail toward the mound of earth that had once been a building, not knowing why except that there was no other place to go.

For a long time he sat in the mud, his back against what was left of the wall. The wind was cool, but still he could feel the sweat oozing from his skin. When at last he looked back down the trail, Cox was still lying there, facedown. Beyond the corpse, and browsing on a muddy patch of grass, was the black horse that had fled when Cullen struck it. The sight of the animal brought him back to thinking coherently, and he knew Cox's mount must be close by. He got up slowly and circled the sod mound to find the mud-plastered animal tethered to a fencepost, blinking patiently.

Cullen untied him and got into the saddle, then set out to bring back his own mount. Worry over how he would manage to get Cox's body onto a horse clouded his mind, and then he saw a figure in the distance and knew it was Shelly Horn coming toward him afoot. The farmer was slogging along with a dogged determination, and Cullen sighed heavily and rode out in his direction.

"It's me! Frank Cullen!" he bawled with all his strength, wary lest the boy might fire on him, thinking he was Cox. He also took off the straw hat, thinking his gray hair might better identify him.

"Cox!" the boy yelled. "Did you find Cox?"

"I found him," Cullen said. "He's dead, Shelly. Couldn't you catch your horse, son?"

"He went back to our place, I reckon," Shelly said in a choked voice. "I ought to whip you for what you did, Cullen! Cox was *my* lookout."

"You're wrong," Cullen told him tiredly. "But if you've got to whip me, let's get at it. Then you can help me pack the body back to town."

"You're not hit?" Shelly asked wonderingly as he mounted Cullen's black. "And where's your gunbelt?"

"Back there in the mud." Cullen said, nodding. "I killed him with the rifle, not a handgun. Come on. Let's ride. It's coming on to rain again before long."

There was disbelief in Shelly's face. "I thought — "

Cullen spurred away, drowning out the rest of the boy's words. When they reached the place where Cox lay in the trail, Shelly was silent.

Together they retrieved Cullen's gunbelt, then heaved the body across the rump of Cullen's horse, arms and legs dangling loosely. With no rope to tie it securely, the body shifted with the motion of the horse, and Cullen had to ride with a hand on the small of Cox's back, feeling the flesh grow cold as the blood drained slowly to stain the horse's flanks and dribble off into the trail below.

He left Shelly at the Horn place. When Marcy came out to call to him her cry was cut off by the sight of the horse's load. With a rope, they lashed the corpse down, then Cullen got into his own saddle.

"Go on home, Marcy," he told his daughter. "Your mother is worried. You tell her — " He left off, but she would know what to tell Emily. Enough, anyway, for now. The sun was already blotted out behind the gray wall of cloud, and rain was falling again as Cullen started the last leg of his journey.

He had ridden slowly because there seemed no point in haste, or maybe in deference to the figure doubled across the saddle of the horse trailing him by a rope length. The huddle of soaked buildings that was Trinidad gleamed dully beyond the rushing river. A crew worked doggedly at a rebuilt trestle paralleling the bridge as he crossed. With no emotion, he watched them turn their heads and point at the corpse.

Hatless, soaked through to his skin, Cullen rode down the street into town. The rain had driven everyone indoors except the railroad crew, but two men came out of Gilliam's as Cullen passed. One of them yelled something he didn't catch, and the other ducked inside. Without turning his head he saw the row of faces lining the broad window of the barbershop, and when he finally reined up at the jail he knew there were a dozen men slogging through the mud back of him.

He looped the reins of the black over the tie rail and hauled the other horse in close by the lead rope. Then he stepped around the rail and pushed open the door, almost colliding with Hayes Larrabee.

"Well, Cullen," the big man said. "Come in out of the wet. What are you doing — ?"

Then he spotted Cox through the doorway and his mouth fell open. "Jesus," he whispered.

"It's George Cox," Cullen told him. "Get me a piece of paper and a pen and I'll write out a statement. I shot him with a rifle out by the old stage depot."

"Sure, Cullen. Just give me a minute to get my wind back, will you? This is a crazy business for sure." Larrabee grabbed his hat off a nail and followed Cullen out into the drizzle. A silent knot of men ringed the corpse, staring white-faced at the rain running off Cox's head.

"We was getting up a posse, Cullen," the sheriff said, squatting to study the dead man closely. "Looks like you saved us some trouble — and Cox a rope. All right, men, this ain't no sideshow out here. Get on back to whatever you was at."

"Hell," a rangy nester close by Larrabee said. "The bastard had a lot more coming to him than getting shot! I'd of worked him over with a knife for what he done to the girl!" A muddy boot swung in a short arc and thudded against Cox's shoulders.

"Goddam it, get the hell away from here, Babcock!" Larrabee said hotly. "Cullen, just relax now."

"What are you going to do?" Cullen said

testily, fists balling of their own accord. "Let him hang there all night in the rain?"

"Rain?" Larrabee repeated, as though amused. "I don't reckon the rain makes much mind to him now. Hey, Clay! Get out here and go for the doc. And a couple of you give me a hand with this body." He tugged a knife from his pocket and cut at the knotted ropes that held Cox on the horse.

Cullen turned away weakly and spat. There was something obscene about the whole business, and he was in a hurry to write down what had happened and get back home. By the time he was finished with the scratchy pen, the doctor was there in his capacity of coroner. After Cox had been examined and a blanket pulled over him, Cullen handed the sheriff the statement he had written.

"Thanks, Cullen. There'll be a hearing shortly, but under the circumstances I ain't asking you to stay here till then. Chances are the town'll pin a medal on you anyway. You better go on home. You look beat."

"I am, Larrabee," Cullen said. "I am, for a fact." He had killed two men, three if Hertzog died, and part of him had died with each of them. Right now, though, he had to get back to the ranch and talk to Emily and Marcy.

CHAPTER 16

Cullen and Emily rode to the cemetery back of the wagon with the bodies of Hertzog and George Cox. The teamster had died of complications from the bullet wound in his abdomen the same night Cullen brought Cox in hanging across the saddle. Larrabee rode on the wagon with the undertaker, but no one else stood by as the pine boxes were lowered into the earth. There was no feeling in Cullen for the teamster who had ambushed and killed Jethro Horn, but he blinked and turned away as dirt was shoveled in over George Cox.

"I'm sorry, Frank," Emily said, squeezing his hand softly with hers. "I'm truly sorry. For him — and for you."

"It's all right, Emily. A man can be wrong." He looked beyond the wet mounding earth to other graves. The rain had softened that of Jethro Horn so that now the ground was level there, and it steamed in the warm sun. There were other graves — more than a town like Trinidad seemed to warrant. Head-stones or rude wooden crosses marking the

241

end of lives. There was a tiny marker far from where they stood that once had seemed to end a part of Cullen's life, but the hurt was in the back of his memory now.

"This is a rough land, Frank," Emily said, the sound of her voice tugging him back to the present. "Too many have died violently — I pray this is an end to it."

"It is, Emily. I promise you that much."

"I didn't mean — oh, Frank, the fault wasn't yours. There was no help for what happened. I just thank God I still have you, and that our child is safe and whole."

"I reckon that does it, Frank," Hayes Larrabee said, riding up to them. He took off his hat in deference to Emily, nodding politely. "It was thoughtful of you to come, ma'am."

"We'll be getting back, Sheriff," Cullen told him. After the heavy man had passed, Cullen helped Emily across the ruts and into the buggy. Climbing up beside her, he clucked to the rented team. His wife turned toward him and spoke gently.

"Don't blame yourself, Frank. What's done is done."

They had committed the dead to the earth, but there was new life in that same ground. Nourished by the drenching waters of the downpour, the land was already coming green again. There would be grass for the cattle, to go with the water. Crops would grow, too, Cullen reflected, the memory of Jethro Horn welling up afresh in his mind. *It'll rain again,* the farmer had said with dumb faith, *God looks after his own.*

The softness would go from the ground, and the heat and dust would plague again, but it was true that the rain would always come. Sometimes gently, tauntingly, and again in a rich flood that threatened to drown with its beneficence. With tears flowing, Cullen put an arm around Emily and held her close to him for the rest of the distance back to the town. Neither of them spoke because there was no need for words.

Trinidad looked strangely scrubbed and bright against the faint green that was beginning to touch the hills beyond. The newly built trestle proudly spanned the fast-flowing river, and the twin ribbons of rail it supported trailed into the distance where a smudge of smoke daubed the blue sky.

"Everything is fixed, it seems," Emily said, pointing almost like a child. "The train — see it?"

"I see it, Emily. Deems may be on it, if he's the politician I think he is." He smiled a little ruefully at the way things had worked out.

"Be charitable," she said. "Give the poor

man credit for a kind deed!"

"Paid for with my taxes," Cullen reminded her, but managing a smile.

"Let's race the train to the depot, eh, Emily?"

He had forgotten the condition of the road, and when they pulled up at the depot the train was waiting there, steam sighing impatiently from it and a crown of smoke wreathing the diamond stack. It looked like the whole of Trinidad, and what must have been half the rest of the country, had turned out in Sunday best for the affair.

"Like a circus!" Emily said, her eyes shining. "Or two state fairs. Oh, Frank, Congressman Deems *is* here!"

They made their way through the swarm of people flocking about the freight cars to where their duly elected representative to the Legislature was passing out cigars in an expansive mood, shaking hands, and slapping backs.

"Frank Cullen! Good to see you, Frank! Mrs. Cullen, good day to you and you're prettier than ever. Blessed if you aren't!"

"Hello, Henry," Cullen said, smiling in spite of himself. "You look well fed and pleased with yourself."

"And why not, Frank?" the smooth-shaven, frock-coated man said. "Why not indeed? It isn't every day a man can do so much for his constituents, now is it? There's enough provisions back there to see these folks through the rest of the summer if need be."

"How wonderful!" Emily said, and there were tears in her eyes as she looked up at Cullen. "I'm proud of you both."

"Tell me, Mrs. Cullen," Deems said, leaning close and dropping his voice, "how'd you ever convince this stubborn mule to change his mind?"

"That's the wonderful part of it," she said, taking Cullen's arm. "I didn't have to. It was all his idea."

"Well, he won't regret it. Frank, I'll give you the details in private, but you can forget about those threats to break up the big ranches. For a while anyway. Your going along with the relief measure had a lot to do with it. Have a cigar, and excuse me, folks."

Deems bustled off through the crowd, trailing platitudes and cigars on his way to greet the mayor. Cullen bit the end off the stogie and reached for a match. It was a good cigar.

"You don't mind, Emily?"

"Of course not, dear. At this point I wouldn't mind if you decided to have a drink! Except that this is Sunday, of course. Isn't it wonderful news Deems brought from Austin?"

"Fine," Cullen said wryly. He blew out a plume of smoke and dropped the match into the dirt. "Something for everybody. Next year the farmers may demand the same thing, only more of it. But at the moment, I don't mind a bit, Emily. Like you said, this really is a circus."

"Let's pray they *won't* need help by then," she said. "Frank, we'd better find Marcy, don't you think?"

They found her on the edge of the crowd with the doctor's wife, face lit up like a child's with excitement. She kissed Cullen right in front of Zona Carter, and the woman laughed at his discomfiture.

"You're embarrassing your daddy," she said, and then reached for Emily's hands as though she hadn't seen her for months.

"I don't care!" Marcy said. "I'm proud of him and I don't mind who knows it! And isn't Congressman Deems the cutest little man? Why, you'd think he personally paid for all that food and seed they're unloading."

"That's his job, child," Mrs. Carter said. "Now suppose we all go home and eat something before church. You did plan to stay, of course?"

Cullen felt Emily stiffen alongside of him, and for a moment he was going to say they had to get back to the ranch. Then he shrugged and patted her hand. He had made greater concessions than that, and if it would make Emily and Marcy happy he could do one more thing.

"Lead the way," he said. "We'll be trampled if we stay here, I'm afraid."

Sitting in the pew and listening to Reverend Burton's sermon, Cullen had a hard time remembering that it was such a short time since he'd sat here vowing never to return. The thin, shrill voice was the same, and outside the sky was much like it had been then. The choir sounded just as he remembered it, and when he tried to find the notes of the hymns his voice wouldn't fit.

But *something* was changed. The atmosphere of the church; the feeling about them. Cullen wondered if he himself had changed. He listened to the preacher give thanks to God for the rain and for the benevolence of the government in Austin. For the courage of certain members in the congregation in bearing up under tragic loads.

His daughter caught his eye, and his face softened in response with pride and love for the girl. When she looked down, and then sidewise at the slender boy to her right, Cullen looked too at Shelly Horn. Still not understanding the tenacity of these stubborn-minded nesters, he could admire them nevertheless. In the last few days Cullen had thought much about young Horn, and the idea that had come forth still startled him. Marcy was stubborn, too. It took some swallowing, but Cullen had managed.

The service was over almost before he was ready, and they were standing for the benediction richly given by Congressman Deems. As they moved slowly toward the door, people spoke to Cullen and Emily. People who had kept their eyes turned away in earlier days. There were still those who did that now, and might never change. All was not sweetness and light, but it was noticeably different.

There was a warmth in the handshakes that Cullen found himself admitting he liked, much as he had liked eating chicken dinner with the doctor and Zona Carter. Maybe a man could lose a battle now and then and still win out in the long haul.

"God is great in His forgiveness," the preacher said, taking Cullen's hand in both of his. "I know He will forgive those of us who misjudged you. Come back again, won't you, Frank?"

"I will," Cullen told him, surprised that the man's shrill voice barely grated on him now. "That was a well-put sermon, Reverend."

"Daddy!" Marcy's voice came to him as they stepped outside, and he and Emily turned to see the girl coming to them, still in the black choir robe. Shelly Horn was right back of her, a strained, almost scared look on his freckled face. "We want to talk to you," Marcy added.

"The singing was lovely," Emily said, reaching out to take the boy's hand. "We enjoyed it so much."

"Daddy," Marcy said, and suddenly her cheeks colored vividly and she bit her lip nervously. "We — Shelly and I — "

"I'm way ahead of you, child," Cullen said, patting her on the shoulder. "Why don't you and your mother go along with the doctor and Mrs. Carter while Shelly and I have a talk? Emily?"

"Frank," his wife said, wrinkles creasing her forehead. "Don't be too rough."

"Don't you worry, Emily. You two just run along now. I think Shelly and I can get along without you for a bit."

"All right," she said dubiously. "Come, Marcy. I gather we're not wanted."

"Mr. Cullen," the boy said as soon as the women had moved out of earshot. "It's about me and Marcy. We — "

He blushed to his ears and broke off as someone passing tittered. Cullen laughed in spite of himself, then reached out to take the boy's arm. A man is never a bigger fool than when he goes to another man to ask for a girl they both love.

"This is no place for privacy, Shelly," he said. "Suppose we find a little quieter spot for this discussion."

"Yes, sir," the boy said. His collar seemed to have gotten too tight. "Where should we go?"

Cullen looked up and down the street, puzzled himself, until he saw the doors of Gilliam's bar swing out. He motioned in that direction. "Not as reverent as church for a Sunday, maybe, but — "

Shelly swallowed, then nodded violently. He was like a man clutching at straws, and Cullen wondered if the boy had been that afraid in the dark outside his soddy, in the depot when he turned his back on Cox, or approaching the ambush at the stage station.

Together they walked along the board sidewalk toward Gilliam's. Two of Cullen's riders came out of the bar as they approached. They spoke to Cullen, but eyed the nester curiously. From across the street, Gentry, the lawyer, called a greeting.

"Everybody loves everybody today," Cullen said as they went into the saloon.

"Yes, sir," Shelly said, wetting his lips.

Cullen wondered if this was the first time the boy had gone into a barroom and decided it was. "It's a change from killing, isn't it?" Shelly added.

"That's a point," Cullen admitted, chastened. "That corner table all right, do you think?"

"It's fine with me, sir. You take your choice." Shelly was looking around furtively as if he thought the preacher would suddenly jump out from behind a door.

They sat down and Cullen shuffled his feet easily in the sawdust. Emily would let him hear about this, but he could think of no better place for men to talk. And a beer would taste good.

"You put your mother and sisters on the train east yesterday, I hear," he said, wanting to get that part of it out of the way.

"That's right. Ma couldn't stand staying any longer. And Trissa — after what happened — "

"I understand. I'm sorry, Shelly. I hope you know that."

"Thanks, Mr. Cullen." The boy traced a repetitious design on the table in front of him. "And thanks for what you did. Cox could have killed you, you know."

"Well, he didn't." Cullen glanced at the bar to see Gilliam coming toward them.

"Shelly, I need a foreman on X-R."

"I know. I heard some fellows say you'd likely give the job to Forbes. I'm sorry it was your own foreman you had to kill."

"How about you, Shelly? Think you could run a ranch?"

It stunned the boy. Then Gilliam was there, grinning down at Cullen.

"Teaching him bad habits, Frank," he chided. "A saloon on Sunday? Tsk, tsk!"

"All right, I am." Cullen told the bartender. "I'll buy him a beer, too, if he says so. I know I want one."

"Fine. But I'll buy these," Gilliam said. "I owe Shelly one. Remember, son?"

"Yes, I — Maybe a beer *would* help," Shelly decided. "I don't seem to be able to hear right today."

"Two beers," Gilliam said. "Make yourselves at home, gentlemen."

"I can say it pretty plain, Shelly," Cullen told him, leaning his elbows on the table and looking straight at the boy. "I can't run the place alone. George Cox was my right hand. I guess maybe you know I thought someday Marcy would marry him. Marcy had a mind of her own, though. Thank the Lord."

"Yes, sir. She's a wonderful girl, Marcy is. I don't know why she ever looked at me twice." Shelly studied the designs he was still tracing carefully.

"I'm beginning to understand it," Cullen said. "You were planning to ask for my daughter's hand, I think. I'm asking you to take over as foreman on X-R when you're my son-in-law."

"Mr. Cullen. I'm not a cowman, I'm a farmer," Shelly said. "Why, I couldn't — "

"Hell, you can ride a horse. You can shoot. You've got more guts than most. It won't be easy, but if I thought you were looking for something easy, I wouldn't be here now."

"Two beers. Compliments of Gilliam's!" The bartender set the glasses down with a sweeping flourish. "It's a pleasure having you gentlemen grace the establishment!"

"Thanks, Ramsey," Cullen said. "We'll be back."

"Yes, thanks, Mr. Gilliam. Thanks a lot for everything." Shelly lifted his glass like a man surveying a dose of poison, and Cullen laughed.

"To both of us saying yes," he said. "It won't kill you, boy."

"I didn't say yes, Mr. Cullen. I appreciate your giving me the benefit of the doubt, but even if I could make a foreman for you I'm still a farmer. This year I'll make my first crop in Trinidad. By Christmas I'll be wanting Marcy to be my wife."

"You can marry her now," Cullen said with exasperation. "Don't be a fool, son. The ranch will be yours one day!"

"That's just it, it *wouldn't* be mine. Not like our section is mine. Mr. Cullen, Marcy and I — we talked it all over. She wants it this way too. I'm sorry, but that's the way it is."

Cullen set his glass down so hard that beer sloshed onto the table and ran in a little river to spill over the edge. Shelly blinked and frowned.

"I'll be damned! I really will." Cullen exploded. "You nesters always have been a stupid, stiff-necked bunch. Will you tell me why, for God's sake?"

"I'll try," Shelly said. He swallowed, Adam's apple working over the tight collar. "If I was to offer you a thousand-acre farm with a barn full of milk cows, a henhouse, and a pigsty, would you give up ranching?"

"Give up ranching? Hell, no, I wouldn't. But — " Then slowly the truth came to Cullen, and for a long moment he sat fighting down his anger at the boy across from him. Misfits, he had called them. Fools with no business in a forbidden land. But this was no fool he talked to now.

For twenty years Cullen had dreamed, and

now the dream was wavering in his mind. And yet you could lose without really losing, he thought for the second time that day. He and Emily had carved out a land from heat and dust; what difference now if that land took a different shape from the one he had hoped for? A man could be wrong, just so he found out in time.

"Drink your beer, Shelly," he said. "You're a stupid, red-necked farmer, but you're a good man. A damned good man."

"You mean — it's all right about Marcy and me?"

"I didn't raise an idiot," Cullen said patiently. "And I don't guess my daughter would marry one. Now drink your beer and let's go tell those women they can stop worrying, eh?"

THORNDIKE PRESS hopes you have enjoyed this Large Print book. All our Large Print titles are designed for easy reading, and all our books are made to last. Other Thorndike Large Print books are available at your library, through selected bookstores, or directly from the publisher. For more information about current and upcoming titles, please call or mail your name and address to:

THORNDIKE PRESS
PO Box 159
Thorndike, Maine 04986
800/223-6121
207/948-2962